THE BURIED TREASURE CODES

A BEN BAXTER MYSTERY

RICHARD SKINNER

JELLY BEAN BOOKS · CARDIFF
2023

The right of Richard Skinner to be identified as the
Author of the Work has been asserted by him in accordance
with the Copyright, Designs and Patents Act 1988.

Editor: Will Rees
Editorial: Shaun Russell

Printed and bound in the UK by
4edge, 22 Eldon Way, Hockley, Essex, SS5 4AD

ISBN: 978-1-915439-74-1

Published by
Jelly Bean Books, Mackintosh House
136 Newport Road, Cardiff, CF24 1DJ
www.candyjarbooks.co.uk

For Patrick, Martyn and Charles

THANKS GO to Darby, Daniel and Kate for help with the illustrations and thanks go to Maggie and Martyn Skinner for checking the content, Jill Forbes for checking the English and Irena Wasilewska for useful edditorial sugestions. Thanks also go to Alistair McKinnon for technical help and my wife Maggie, for help with the quilted bag. Thanks also go to the Civil Service Insurance Society for advice on insurance matters, and finally thanks to Candy Jar Books for their editorial contributions.

Friday 11th February

I have rather neglected writing my diary during the last month. We had some American relations staying after Christmas. They wanted to do lots of sightseeing so Mum, my sister Katie and I took them on visits to London, York and Cardiff. Of course, these trips had to be fitted around school. Now that things have quietened down I have dug my big bumper diary back out and intend to begin writing it again.

It was given to me by Katie as a birthday present last July when I turned eleven. The diary's pages were blank, leaving me to fill in the dates as I go along. In this way several pages can be devoted to a single day's goings on, or days can be missed out altogether if nothing much happened. Katie is thirteen and we have a cocker spaniel named Millie and a pet sparrow called Chippy.

We have had Chippy for over eight months now. Katie and I rescued him when we found him fallen out of his nest as a fledgling. We fed him round the clock, with suitable feeds we found listed on the Internet. Since then he has preferred to stay living with us; it may be the cake crumbs that we give him! He has a nest on a top shelf in my bedroom. He flies outside whenever he feels like it, as I leave a window open. Millie is good with Chippy and even lets him land on her back. He sometimes does this if he feels threatened by a larger bird, or else he settles on my shoulder for protection.

We were loaned Millie by the police on a long-term basis. She is an ex-police dog. The police thought we would be able give her a good home after she suffered an injury due to the actions of a vicious criminal. Her job prior to that was as a sniffer dog, checking luggage and packing cases for drugs and other illegal items. We were given her because the police guessed we would find her useful since Katie and I, together with my friend Johnny, have helped them to solve a number of crimes.

This all started when an aunt gave me a book called *The Junior Detective Manual*. It was by an ace detective named Ricky Barton. Johnny and I found it dead cool and immediately set out to try our hands at being store detectives.

Unfortunately, a real store detective thought we had been stealing sweets and arrested us. The police were called and our pockets searched, but they soon realised it had all been a mistake. The police inspector concerned ran us home in his car, which was quite exciting. On the way home he gave us some friendly advice, which set us on the road to actually helping solve one or two small local crimes. I joined a Neighbourhood Watch Group, and Johnny, Katie and I helped solve some small crimes that had been worrying them. One was to do with a sudden spate of cats being stolen, but most of the crimes we have been involved in since were of a more serious nature. In addition, we uncovered what lay behind a ghost who seemed to be haunting a local vicarage on stormy nights.

Millie and Chippy have both helped us with many of our crime-busting escapades. How can a sparrow help? Well, I am sure this will be explained as I continue writing this diary.

Saturday 12th February

My auntie Maudie popped in this morning with some exciting news. She has won a prize for writing the best limerick for a women's magazine. You know the sort of thing: "There was an Australian in Ealing, who walked around on his ceiling..." And so on.

Anyway, the prize is a surprise one and Auntie is expecting it to be delivered tomorrow. I wonder what it will be. Perhaps it will be a non-stick saucepan or a bread maker?

Sunday 13th February

Just after we had had our lunch we heard a strange hooting noise outside our house. Looking out of the window we noticed an orange-coloured camper van parked outside. Out stepped Auntie with the biggest smile imaginable on her face.

'This is my prize!' she told us. 'It's a classic vintage camper van. It's just been overhauled. Rather a beauty, isn't it? Like all camper vans it has a name, which is printed on the front wings.'

We looked and could see the name 'Connie' painted in black on the side of the camper.

'Yes, Connie the Camper Van,' Auntie confirmed.

'Yay!' Katie cried. 'It looks just like a Connie.'

Katie couldn't wait to climb in and inspect the mini kitchen. It was well equipped with a cooker, sink, draining board, cupboards and places to hang your tea towels.

Mum wanted to inspect the sleeping arrangements. The daytime couches folded down to form beds. It was certainly all very well designed and compact.

I climbed into the front and inspected the driving controls. I pretended I was driving and turned the steering wheel. Unfortunately, I could not reach the pedals. I'm looking forward to when I am older and can have a go at driving it properly!

Auntie Maudie suggested we go for a spin

around town, so we all climbed in (me in the front as I was already there!)

It drove very smoothly, although Auntie Maudie found it a bit slow compared to her elderly Vauxhall Cavalier.

'What will you do with your old car now you have this?' Mum asked.

'It will have to go, I'm afraid,' Auntie replied. 'In any case, I was warned by my garage last year that it would not pass its annual MOT next time. They said it needed a lot of money spent on it. They quoted me a price to fix it which was more than the car was worth. So I had already decided to part with it this year. Its MOT is due later this month, so the arrival of Connie is a godsend.'

'Yes, now you have this beautiful camper van, you can happily say goodbye to your old car,' Mum commented.

'Actually, I will be sad to get rid of my Cavalier. It has been my faithful runabout for fifteen years. Still, this camper has arrived with perfect timing,' Auntie Maudie replied.

Monday 14th February

It's half term this week – so no school until next Monday!

Johnny came round and we played computer games on my new (to me) Progax 4. I have two controllers, so we raced each other round a Silverstone track on my vintage sportscar game. Johnny is pretty good. I think he plays a lot of computer games at home. We won three games each. The person with the old Cooper Bristol usually lost to the Supercharged Bentley. We took it in turns to race each car.

After lunch Johnny called again and we took Millie for a walk in the park. Chippy came as well, flying from tree to tree on the way. He likes to shelter in trees and watch out for larger birds. Birds like magpies scare him, with good reason. They are quite territorial and can object to small birds entering their patch.

Tuesday 15th February

Today Johnny and I went for a last ride in Auntie Maudie's old Vauxhall Cavalier.

'The best price you will get for this old car of yours will be at Jim's Scrapyard,' the garage man had told her. 'They can take it apart and sell the parts as spares for repairing similar old cars.'

So that is where we went today.

The scrap-yard was full of cars of all ages which were being taken apart. Useable items, such as gearboxes and even engines, if still good enough, were being removed. These would then be sold to people whose own cars needed such items replacing.

Whilst Auntie Maudie was discussing how much Jim would give her for her car, we asked if we could have a look at the cars in the yard. Jim said we could, provided we were careful.

'There are some jagged bits of metal lying around, so keep an eye out and watch where you tread,' he told us. Auntie Maudie was a bit worried by this, but could see we were keen to look at the old cars.

She said, 'Just be careful, boys, and don't be too long. I'll need to get a taxi to take us back home before long.'

Jim told her he would get one of his engineers to run us home, as it was not far, so there was no great need for us to hurry.

Johnny and I spotted a car which looked much too good to be scrapped. We had a close look at it then climbed into it. It was really quite posh, with red leather seats and the dashboard and doors finished in polished mahogany.

Johnny looked in the glove compartment and found an old booklet headed 'Owner's Manual'.

'This looks rather interesting,' he said. 'Wow! And look at this page I've found near the back. It's got a lot of very strange writing on it. It's all handwritten, perhaps by its previous owner. It doesn't make any sense to me.'

I had a look and told him it might be some foreign language or possibly a secret coded message. And then on the next page I noticed there was a roughly drawn map with a place marked with a cross on it.

'It's certainly very mysterious,' I said. 'I wonder who's behind all this and why?'

Johnny replied, 'Mysteries are what we look into. I reckon we should see if we can buy this booklet from Jim and spend some time seeing what it means, especially if it *is* a coded message.'

I agreed and added, 'If it *is* a coded message someone has spent quite a bit of time on it. Why would anyone go to all that trouble without a good reason? It's certainly very strange!'

I took several photos of the car and other vehicles of interest. Then we headed back to the office. We showed Jim the owner's manual we had found and asked him if we could purchase it, as it looked interesting. He took the booklet and looked at it briefly.

'Oh, you found this in that old Jaguar out there?'

'That's right,' Johnny replied.

'Ha, well, that car belonged to one of the notorious London criminal gangs, the Trinder brothers. Charlie Trinder was the actual owner. He bought it back in 1963. It's a 3.4 litre Mk 2 Jag. This was a very popular model with the criminal fraternity in those days. It could outpace most police cars. It could do well over a ton, that is to say, over one hundred miles per hour. Both brothers died a long time ago in a car crash. They were driving brother Reggie's car at the time, a similar Jaguar. This one was then passed down to Charlie's son. He has had it hidden away in a lockup garage for over forty years. He was ashamed of his dad's criminal past and rarely used it. Due to recent illness, he has decided it's time to get rid of it. He brought the car in just the other day. He said I could have the car for spare parts, but on no account was I to sell it in one piece for restoration. He did not want his dad's favourite car placed in a museum for people to gloat over and to glorify his dad's criminal history. That is what he told me. So it has to be taken apart and the parts sold, the same as will now happen to your aunt's old Vauxhall.

'Going back to the owner's manual you found, I don't see why you shouldn't have it. I've got to get rid of the vehicle piece by piece, after all. What would you say to paying one pound for it?'

We agreed at once to paying a pound and found him the cash.

Smiling, Jim said, 'I'll give you a receipt to make the sale quite legal.'

On the way home Johnny whispered to me, 'Did you notice that car's registration?'

'Yes,' I said, 'it was CAT101.'

'Do you think the owner was a cat burglar?' Johnny asked, with a cheeky grin on his face.

'Very good,' I replied. One of our earliest mysteries involved disappearing cats!

When we got back to my house, Johnny and I had a further look at the manual. Inside the front, it had the owner's name, Charles Anthony Trinder, and his old address in Hackney, London. And at the back, on some blank pages left for the owner's own notes, one page was covered with the strange set of letters we had seen earlier. The following page had a map of some kind drawn on it. It seemed to be for a place out in the countryside, mainly consisting of parkland with some woodland to the north, a pond and some footpaths. It didn't say where it was. It could have been anywhere; it was so lacking in detail. On the following page there were some handwritten notes, left, we supposed, by Mr Trinder. They told us something about the car giving offence and going to an island. It was written in plain English, but didn't seem to make a lot of sense.

As for the weird text, it was completely unintelligible. I have attached a photograph of it below in my diary.

'Do you think it's a foreign language like Russian

or Swedish?' Johnny wondered.

'I don't think it's Russian, they write using Cyrillic script which has Ns and Rs written backwards and other letters not found in our alphabet. I read about it for a language project at school,' I told him. 'If you notice this message or whatever it is, it's all written in capitals and there's no punctuation.'

'Wait a minute,' Johnny muttered, 'there are several full stops, which might be important. Why don't we see if Katie has any thoughts about what it might be?'

Katie was in her room doing homework, but stopped what she was doing when we came in.

We showed her the old Jaguar owner's manual and explained that we had found it when we had gone with Auntie Maudie to a scrapyard to get rid of her old Vauxhall.

'It was in a car which apparently belonged to a member of a notorious London criminal gang – the Trinder brothers. It was purchased by a Charlie Trinder back in the 1960s,' I told her. 'We noticed this strange writing on one of its pages meant for "Notes", and asked the scrap-yard dealer if we could buy it from him. He agreed, so here it is.

NOTES

```
FSEENHSYLOSIHLOHYEZTBIAU8
5IE.OAKPGITBLNBNOYUTTFZIUE
T3OTST.RFEIWLMUIIEGTSGBHUI
SRDS53HGS.WH1YDFAPNIBLITED
AR3RFMTVLGEUBO.IIOASECOTNA
ENRAMSEYDRIREIDSTYM.TNORO
XTIFDLRAENEU2ASOTALNUOHC
P.AISXENEETSSGSRYEODAPSOO
OELEOOC1O.STSTNCSEHMSEFAO
SUIVAENATRAURWA9.SIIEIHDP
IEAIONNHLHESDTNHPCPDNT8.
```

What do you think these letters mean?' She looked at the writing, and after some thought, she said, 'I don't think it's a foreign language. If it is, it is very unpronounceable-looking, with things like TTFZIU in it. It looks to me like a coded message. Goodness knows what it means. It looks very complicated. You might have to get a professional codebreaker to sort it out.'

I told her we should perhaps keep it to ourselves

for the time being. 'If any present-day criminals who knew the Trinders learn about it, we could be in trouble. First we need to see if we can find a key to breaking this code ourselves.'

'Mmm,' she replied. 'A bit more sleuthing coming up, I can see!'

'It could actually be quite a simple code,' she added. 'If you can discover what type of code it is, and there are many different types, you might be able to solve it yourselves. You could look it up on the Internet, but it would be more fun to go to the library. They must have books about code breaking. You might find examples of the different common codes. If you can identify which this one is, and I'm pretty sure it is a coded message, at least that would be a start. I'd take a closer look, but I have to finish my homework now.'

We left her in peace. By now it was almost teatime, so we had to put off any visits to the library until tomorrow.

Wednesday 16th February

Johnny and I went to the library this morning in search of a book about code breaking. There were not many other people in there. The lady in charge asked if she could help us. We told her we were interested in codes and code breaking. I made out it was for a school project. I know this was a bit of a lie, but I didn't want her to know too much about what we were up to. She seemed impressed by our interest in this subject and told us that she had only recently found out that her mother had been a code breaker. Her wartime job had, apparently, been helping people to break German secret codes.

'It was so secret that I didn't find out about it until years later,' she said. 'She only told me when it became de-classified information. This meant that our government had decided that this information, once so very secret, was no longer considered so.'

Luckily, the code breakers her mother was helping got hold of one of the machines that the Germans used to code most of their messages. This helped them work out how to tackle the problem of unscrambling the coded messages.

'Unless you know what type of code is being used, it is almost impossible to unscramble a message,' she told us. 'The place where my mother worked was called Station X. It was located at Bletchley Park, Buckinghamshire, in the early 1940s.

She could have told you all you need to know if she was still alive. You can go there nowadays, as they now have a museum on the site. During the war, they developed a computer to help solve the complex German codes. For your school project it would be worth going to the museum to learn all about code breaking. You would see one of the Enigma machines which the Germans used for coding their secret messages. They also have a model of the "bombe", the computer I mentioned which was built to help decipher the enigma messages.'

She then took us to a shelf where there were a couple of books about codes. One was for young children and showed some simple codes. The other looked more comprehensive, as it went into detail about the history of coded messages and showed how they worked. We decided to take out both of these.

When we got back to my house, we sat down and had a look at these books. Johnny took the more elementary one to look at. There was an introduction about a couple of words which were useful when talking about coded messages:

'Plain text': This is a message in plain English.

'Cipher text': A plain text message which has been put into code.

In my diary, for simplicity, I will call all coded messages just that: 'coded messages'.

A common type of code shown in the library books is called the substitution code. There are twenty-six letters in the English alphabet. With this type of code, each letter is substituted with a different letter to produce the coded message. The simplest way of doing this is to replace each letter in the alphabet with the letter which comes after it. In other words, A is replaced with B, B with C and so on for the whole alphabet, with Z being replaced with A at the end.

'To decode this type of coded message the process is reversed, and each coded letter is replaced with the letter coming before it in the alphabet,' the book read.

'Let's try this simple substitution with our coded message,' Johnny suggested.

'Okay,' I agreed, 'let's just try the first ten letters to see if this bit of message makes any sense. There's no need to do it for the whole message. If the first bit makes sense, we can then do the rest.'

To help us read this code we wrote down the alphabet from A to Z on a sheet of paper.

A B C D E F G H I J K L M N
O P Q R S T U V W X Y Z

The first ten letters of the coded message in the owner's manual were F S E E N H S L Y O. Replacing each letter with the one before it in the alphabet, F became E, S became R and so on. In this way the coded message from the Jaguar became E R D D M G R K X N. This obviously made no sense at all, so we tried some other simple substitutions. One was swapping the alphabet with a backwards alphabet. In other words, A B C when coded became Z Y X. This and several other simple methods all proved equally useless.

'It could be a more complex type of substitution being used,' I suggested. 'From the code book I've been reading, it seems people sometimes use a randomly made-up list of letters to pair with the normal alphabet. For example, this could be something like A replaced by F, B replaced by L, C replaced by H and so on, with no particular order to it. This makes decoding much more difficult. Unless you have a copy of the mixed-up alphabet, which has been paired with the ordinary alphabet, it's not easy to unscramble the coded message.'

'Let's give it up until later,' Johnny suggested. 'Then we can see if we come up with some better ideas.'

I agreed and said, 'I would like to read the code books in more detail, especially what they have to say about solving the more complicated substitution codes.'

So we put on our coats and took Millie and Chippy to the park.

I have just had my supper and am going to look at my library code book in more detail. It describes how, back in 1585, Mary Queen of Scots, a cousin of Queen Elizabeth I, used substitution coded messages. She used these to send and receive secret messages to and from her Catholic friends. They were plotting to get rid of Queen Elizabeth. The system she used was rather more complicated than the usual substitution setup. As well as having a letter to replace each of the twenty-six letters of the English alphabet, they added more code symbols. Some were dummy ones meaning nothing at all and had to be ignored; a few others stood for whole words such as 'and' and 'the'. This made deciphering her messages almost impossible.

Mary felt confident that her messages were completely undecipherable and agreed to help plan the assassination of Queen Elizabeth. Unbeknownst to her, Queen Elizabeth's men had employed a very skilful man named Thomas Philippes, who was, as Johnny would say, 'a cool dude' when it came to code breaking. It took him some time to decipher the first few coded messages, but once the code had been broken, later messages were easy to read. The result was that Mary Queen of Scots was found guilty of plotting against the English monarch and executed.

My code book explains that if the code used is a

substitution type, there is a method which helps to find which letters have been paired with those of the normal alphabet, to produce a coded message. Thomas Philippes apparently used this and other tricks to decipher Mary Queen of Scots' messages. It involves looking at how often each letter is used in a coded message. Or to put it another way, checking how frequently each letter is used.

In plain English, it has been found that E is the most commonly used letter. Next comes the letter T, with A, and O, coming close behind. The least common letters used are J, Q, X, and Z.

Based on looking at many hundred pieces of text from books, newspapers and so on, people have come up with the typical frequency with which each letter occurs. That is how many times each letter is found in every hundred letters used.

Out of every one hundred letters, the letter E occurs typically thirteen times. T occurs nine times, A eight times and O just over seven times. It follows that the most common letter found in a coded message is likely to equal the letter E in the original message. And the least common letters found are likely to represent J, Q, X, or Z.

As this is all getting a bit complicated and I'm feeling rather tired, I'm going to leave any further reading about codes until tomorrow.

Thursday 17th February

This morning I spent more time studying my library code book. As noted last night, the most common letter found in a coded message is likely to represent an E in the original plain text message. The next most common one probably replaces T, and so on for all the letters in the coded message. In this way it should be possible to decode the whole of a coded message.

Unfortunately, this method does not work well for short messages. A coded message apparently needs to contain a thousand or more letters for it to work with any degree of accuracy. As our coded message looks a lot shorter than this, we might not be able to decipher it. Nevertheless, I have decided to try it. This may, with a bit of luck, give some idea of what some bits of the message mean, and we might then be able to guess the rest.

Our coded message also has some numbers in it, like the number eight, which comes at the very end. I have decided that for the present I will ignore these.

At this point Johnny came round and I told him what I had learnt from my book.

'So, what do we do now?' he asked.

'How would you like to take our coded message and note down how many times each letter occurs in it, working from A to Z?'

He agreed to do this whilst I went and found him a fizzy drink.

Whilst I was downstairs, Mum asked me to run a short errand for her, taking a note to old Mrs Skelton round the corner. When I returned, I asked Johnny how he had got on with his counting.

'I've finished,' he told me. He showed me his findings. He had found eighteen As, six Bs, seven Cs and so on for the whole alphabet. He had also counted the total number of letters used in the coded message. There were 253. He had ignored any numbers found, as instructed by me beforehand.

'What next?' Johnny asked.

'Well I noticed in my code book that they recommend drawing up a bar chart using our findings, then comparing it with one based on plain texts.

'You what!?' he exclaimed. 'I've never heard of a bar-whatever-it-was-you-said.'

'That doesn't surprise me,' I replied. 'We've only just done them in our maths class at school. I'll show you what they are like using the numbers you've just counted.'

I took out a piece of paper which had squares printed on it and wrote A, B, C and so on, up to Z along the bottom. Then, above the letter A, I counted eighteen squares up and hatched them in with a black pen; above B, I hatched in six squares up. I repeated the process for each of the twenty-six letters he had counted. The result was a series of hatched-in bars above each letter. I have copied the drawing into my diary below. The tallest bar represented the most common letter found and the shortest the least common.

When I had finished, Johnny wanted to know what it all meant. 'You've produced an interesting diagram,' he told me, 'but how does it help us?'

'Well, my library book tells me that we should compare this chart with a similar chart based on how often each letter of the alphabet is found in plain English text. They have kindly included a list of how often each letter occurs in plain text, based on thousands of words found in books, newspapers and magazines.'

'Wow, that must have taken some hours to count!' he replied.

'I expect they used a computer program for that,' I told him. 'I dare say if I had the right program on my computer, I could have very rapidly done all the counting you have just completed!'

So I drew a second chart underneath the one I had already drawn, showing how often each letter occurs in plain text. This made it easy to compare the two charts.

The two charts are shown below. The top chart is for the numbers found by Johnny, counting each letter in our coded message. The bottom chart is for the frequency each letter is found in plain English.

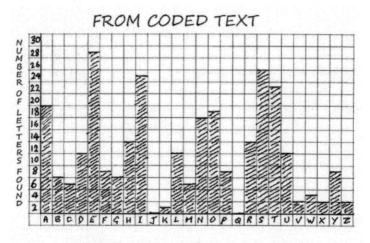

FROM CODED TEXT

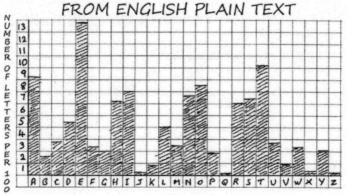

FROM ENGLISH PLAIN TEXT

I had explained to Johnny earlier that, in plain English, E was the most common letter used. The bottom chart, based on plain English, clearly confirmed this: E had the tallest bar above it. Strangely enough, in the chart above, based on the coded message, E also had the tallest bar above it.

This would suggest that if a substitution code was being used, then E had been replaced with itself. This was very odd. The library code book indicated that no letters would normally be coded with themselves.

However, in case the person designing the code (Mr Trinder) had purposely paired E with itself to confuse anyone trying to decode the message, we continued to compare the heights of all the bars in both charts.

Our conclusion was that the two charts looked extremely similar. As already noted, E was the most common letter, with the tallest bars found in both charts. J, Q, X, and Z were by far the least common letters in both charts. There were small differences for some of the other letters. For example, in plain English, T is the second most common letter found. In the coded message it was the fourth most common letter, but it still occurred very frequently. The letter I was found more frequently than A in the coded message, whereas in plain English text it would have been the other way around. But these differences were small.

We agreed that, basically, the two charts looked almost identical. If a substitution code had been used, we would not have expected this.

'It's very peculiar,' Johnny commented. 'It looks

as if our message has not been coded and yet it's unreadable!'

'There are other kinds of code,' I said. 'The substitution type is not the only kind. Looking at my library code book last night I found one which could fit the bill. The letters in the plain text message are simply rearranged in a different order.'

'That sounds like an old TV sketch I once watched,' Johnny said. 'There was that comedian, Eric somebody or other, he played some music on a piano. On being told it was completely wrong, his answer was that he had played all the right notes, *but not necessarily in the right order*!'

'Yes,' I said, laughing, 'I saw that one in a programme of repeats recently. And that exactly mirrors the type of code I was referring to. It's called "rail fence transposition". It uses all the correct letters, but mixes them up into a different order.'

'Wow, it sounds as if we're going to have an impossible task trying to solve our coded message. If that type of code has been used, how on earth will we unjumble it?' Johnny asked.

'Well, rail fence coding uses a fairly simple system of mixing up the letters. This makes it reasonably easy to reverse the mixing and get to the plain text message,' I told him.

'Hold on a minute,' Johnny said, '"rail fence" rings a bell with me. Did you see that note scribbled on a page of the owner's manual? It follows the sketch-map. Mr Trinder has written something which mentioned rail, and I have a feeling fence also came into it. I had no idea what he was talking about when I read it. Now it's beginning to make sense.'

'Let's have another look,' I said.

Johnny thumbed open the manual. 'Yes, here it is. It says, "If this car causes much more offence I will travel to the island of treasure by rail".' Do you think "offence" could be a hint for the word "fence"? Then couple it with the word "rail". Could it be pointing us to a rail fence type of code?'

'I think you may well be right,' I replied. 'Full marks for spotting those clues, but I don't know what the island of treasure bit has got to do with it.'

At this point Katie poked her head around my bedroom door and asked how we were getting on with breaking the code.

I showed her the bar charts we had produced.

'Oh, very impressive,' she remarked. 'Who showed you how to draw bar charts?'

'Mrs Bennet, our maths teacher,' I told her.

'Oh yes, I know her,' Katie replied. 'She only started at our school last year, I've heard she is very good.'

'Yes, we've also done pie charts,' I told her.

Johnny, of course, thought this must be to do with food and asked, 'Can you eat them?'

Katie rolled her eyes and shook her head. 'Johnny, you are being silly!' she told him. 'Mrs Bennet is a maths teacher. It's nothing to do with cookery. Anyway, what do your bar charts show?'

She studied them in more detail and noticed, as we had, that the letter E was the most common one in both the coded message and plain English text.

'That's funny,' she commented. 'Most people would avoid using the same letters when coding a message. The patterns of peaks and troughs in both charts are very similar. Looking at the two charts, anyone would think the unreadable coded message had not been coded.'

'Johnny and I have decided that Mr Trinder's message is almost certainly not based on a substitution type of code, because of what the bar charts show us,' I told her.

'What other types are there?' she asked.

I told her about the rail fence code, and that Mr Trinder had left a strong hint that this was the type of code he had used. 'Johnny found it on one of the pages in the owner's manual which we found in his old Jag,' I added.

I showed her his message.

'Yes, it does sound as if this might be the type of code to look at,' Katie said. 'I haven't heard of it myself. Good luck, I will leave you two at it.'

However, as it was lunch time, we decided to

leave code solving for later and Johnny went home. I went downstairs to see if lunch was ready.

After lunch I went round to Johnny's house and we raced each other in a car game on his K-box 10 games machine.

It's surprising how the time can fly by when you get absorbed by these games. My auntie Maudie reckons they are a waste of time and boys and girls ought to spend more time outdoors getting exercise.

'They spend far too long sitting hunched over their computers,' she has told me, and she is probably right. 'They will end up with hunched backs and square eyes.'

So Johnny and I decided that after we had had our tea we would meet up and take Millie for a walk; Chippy would no doubt fly along with us.

After tea, although we knew it would be getting dark soon, we decided it was still worth going for a walk. Millie was keen and Chippy also wanted to stretch his wings. He is of course free to fly off on his own whenever he wants. However, he likes to accompany us when we go out. Perhaps he is simply curious to see where we are going, or he likes our company.

We went to the park. Johnny thought he would get some practise at 'shooting from the hip', using his phone camera. We had been told by our policeman friend, Mark, that this was the best way to secretly take photos of suspicious-looking people. 'You never know, they may be criminals,' he told us. He had originally come close to arresting us a while ago, when we were mistakenly thought to be shoplifting at a local store.

We went through the park and Millie ran around stretching her legs. Chippy, who likes to fly from tree to tree, kept a watch on us. He also watches out for larger birds, especially birds of prey. They can pounce on any unsuspecting smaller bird and even the odd pigeon – well, especially pigeons, as they can make a tidy meal for the likes of a sparrow hawk.

However, we didn't see any birds of prey and Chippy was able to fly around happily.

We decided to walk home via a footpath through the adjacent woodland. It was beginning to get dark so I put Millie on her lead. I am especially careful to keep Millie close when we get near the woods. She was kidnapped just over three months ago at the entrance to this woodland. Chippy also decided it was safer sitting on my shoulder. He is more of a daytime sort of bird, and in the twilight hours is less happy at being out and about. Who knows what evil birds may be lurking up in the treetops?

Johnny has got pretty proficient at shooting from the hip when taking photos. He has been practising using me as his target in the park. We had a quick look at his photos when we got to the woods, and he was spot on target most of the time. When he first tried to do this some while ago, he only managed photos of treetops or the ground, but not of the people he was trying to photograph!

As we were leaving the woods and coming onto the road outside, a car pulled up and parked next to the wood's entrance. A man got out, went round to the back of his car, and opened his boot. We were quite close by now. As soon as he saw us, he slammed his boot shut and turned to face away from us. We carried on walking, but before he had closed the boot, we noticed there were quite a few plastic bags and other things in there. His actions seemed very suspicious. However, we were careful to continue on our way, pretending we had not noticed his odd behaviour. When we were just past the car, Johnny looked back and, shooting from the hip, photographed it. We then carried on home.

'I reckon he is going to do some fly-tipping,' I told Johnny.

'That's really terrible,' Johnny replied. 'It leaves a nasty mess, which someone else has to clear up.'

Friday 18th February

Johnny came round early this morning and we decided to visit the park and woods again to see if there had been any overnight fly tipping. If so, we would contact the police and they could see if it could be traced back to the person who had tipped it. It was, we felt, quite likely to be linked to the man with the car Johnny had photographed. He had managed to get at least one good picture of the car, despite it being a bit dark when we had seen it.

Katie had just finished her breakfast, so we told her we were going to take Millie out and asked if she wanted to come along. She said she would come as she had not been out of the house for a couple of days. Her friend Poppy had gone down with flu and Janice, another friend, was away.

We made our way through the park and reached the woods. Chippy as usual flew ahead, going from tree to tree. Millie, who was off the lead, kept close.

We were just telling Katie how we had seen a suspicious man yesterday and were wondering if he had been fly-tipping when we bumped into Colin Jenkins. He is in the same class as Johnny at school. He was carrying a smart ladies' handbag.

Johnny quipped, 'It suits you, Colin!' pointing to the bag.

He replied, 'I've just found it in the woods. There's nothing in it, I looked, but I reckon it will make a nice wedding present for my big sister when she gets married in May.'

Katie looked carefully at the bag. It was a Rudley, as it had their little white elephant pendant hanging from its strap. It looked almost new.

'Where in the woods was it?' I asked him.

Colin pointed to a path going off to the right a little further on.

I told Colin that he should take the bag to the police station, as someone had probably dropped it by mistake.

'Not likely,' he replied. 'Finders keepers!'

'That's quite an expensive bag,' Katie told him. 'Someone will be really sad to have lost it.'

'Well they ain't having it,' Colin replied. 'They should look after their stuff better. Anyway, I need a wedding present and I think this will save me having to spend any pocket money. I will wrap it up and give it to my sister. It looks almost new.'

With that he hurried off the way we had just come.

We made our way in the direction that Colin had indicated he had found the bag.

'Colin doesn't seem a very nice boy,' Katie commented. 'A lady somewhere will be feeling terrible about losing her nice handbag.'

'I know,' Johnny replied, 'Colin is always in trouble at school. He tried stealing our teacher's best pen. Luckily for her she saw him and told him off, warning him it would be a detention next time. He was caught the next day writing rude things about her in chalk on a wall by the bicycle sheds. This time he was given a double detention.'

After we had walked about thirty metres, Millie became very interested in a pile of leaves. She scratched at them and then sat down and looked up at us.

'I think she's found something,' Johnny said.

'What have you found, old girl?' I asked her. She looked at me and gave a little woof.

I poked about with a stick in the leaves where Millie had been sniffing. Sure enough there was something there. It turned out to be another handbag!

I reached down and picked it up. It looked in quite good condition. It couldn't have been in the woods very long as it was perfectly dry and very clean.

I passed it to Katie and she looked inside. 'Wow, it has lots of personal things in it,' she said. 'I can see a compact, lipstick... There's also a wallet. Let's have a look... It's empty. No, wait a minute there's a driving licence in it.'

'We should take it to the police,' I said.

'Before we do so, we ought to check for any fly-tipping,' Johnny suggested. 'That chap last night had quite a lot of plastic bags in his car boot – remember?'

We continued walking and had only gone a short way when Millie discovered yet another ladies' handbag. It was barely hidden. It was lying under just a scattering of leaves by a tree not far off the path.

'This is very weird,' Johnny commented. 'This is the third bag found here so far.'

We hunted around some more and found two more bags. We were becoming weighed down with them. Katie decided the best thing would be to call the police. They could come and collect them and see for themselves if there were still more to be found.

'You're right,' I agreed, taking out my mobile phone.

I phoned Detective Inspector Mark Riley's number. He's the policeman we met last year and is now quite a friend. Luckily for us, he answered his phone straight away. When I told him what we had been uncovering he said, 'Stay where you are, I will be with you in about ten minutes.'

We had a brief further search whilst we waited, and Millie uncovered yet another bag.

I told her she had been a very clever dog and found her a doggy treat. Chippy, who had been up a tree, flew down and I found him some cake crumbs (I always keep a few in a small bag in my pocket). After what seemed ages, we heard footsteps coming through the woodland and Mark Riley appeared, accompanied by a policewoman.

When he saw what we had found he gave a low whistle.

'Well, you have been busy!' he told us.

The policewoman put on a pair of latex gloves and opened some of the bags. Most contained ladies' personal items such as lipstick and hairbrushes. Any purses found were generally empty, and notably there were no mobile phones.

'It looks to me as if this might be the work of our local handbag snatcher,' Mark told us. 'We've recently had a spate of calls from women who have been out shopping and had their bags snatched by man wearing a hood. He cycles up quietly behind them and grabs their bags as he rides past. The ladies have no chance of seeing his face or chasing after him. It leaves them in quite a state of shock.'

I told Mark that we might have spotted the man involved yesterday evening. Johnny had taken a surreptitious photo of him with his mobile phone, while the man had been standing next to his car. Johnny took his phone out and showed Mark the picture he had taken.

'Oh, well done, Johnny,' Mark said. 'This could be especially useful. Even if we can't see the man's face, it shows his car and its number plate very well. I shall need to borrow your phone, but I will pop in to see you later and bring it back. In any case, I will need to speak to you all again. Will this afternoon be suitable?'

Katie said she was sure it would be okay, and Johnny agreed he could come round to our house after he had had his lunch.

Mark told us that he and police officer Barbara Smith would have to take the bags we had found back to the station. They would then get a team of officers to comb the woods for any further bags that may have been dumped.

This afternoon Mark Riley called as promised. We recounted what we had seen the evening before, as we left the woods going onto the adjacent road.

I told Mark, 'The man we saw didn't seem to want us to see his face.'

'Hmm, I wonder why?' Mark murmured. 'With what you say about the bags in the boot, it is all very suspicious. Good work all of you, including Millie, of course. That dog of yours deserves a lot of credit for her sniffing skills.

'We've finished with your phone, Johnny, excellent work on your part too. We've copied out the photos you took. I hope to get information about the car owner's identity shortly.'

'Going back to what was found in the handbags,' I said, 'I was a bit surprised that there were no mobile phones in any of them. Do you think our thief is keeping them to sell?'

'It's quite likely,' Mark replied, 'but there's another possibility. You see, many phones these days can be tracked, and therefore most criminals disable them as soon as they can. Leaving them in the woodland might allow the police to track them there and find the handbags they were in. In doing so they might find clues like fingerprints, revealing the thief's identity.

'So far, by my reckoning you have discovered five bags dumped in the woods?'

'Well, actually there was a sixth bag,' I told him.

'Oh! Where is the sixth?' he asked.

Johnny explained that, as we reached the woods this morning, we had met a classmate of his, Colin Jenkins. He had already found one bag, which he showed us. 'He said he was going to give it to his sister,' Johnny concluded.

'Yes, he told us it was empty,' Katie said, 'but I wonder now if he was telling the truth. The bags we found all had various personal items in them, such as credit cards.'

'I must pay this lad a visit and question him about it,' Mark told us.

Katie said, 'We did say to him he should hand it in at a police station. But he insisted he was going to give it to his big sister as a wedding present, as she is getting married soon.'

'I'm afraid that bag is an important part of a bigger crime. He certainly cannot keep it,' Mark told us. 'I wonder what happened to its contents. I suppose it could have been dumped by our bag-snatcher, but this now seems rather unlikely. Do you know where this Colin Jenkins lives?'

We did not, so Mark decided he would find out by ringing the school secretary as soon as he got back to his office.

'I must go now, but for the time being, please don't tell anybody about your findings in the woods. We don't want lots of people tramping round there hunting for more bags. There may be clues which can help confirm our robber's identity.'

Saturday 19th February

We had another visit from Detective Inspector Mark Riley this morning. Mum was surprised to see him again so soon. 'Hello! Back already?' she said.

'Yes,' Mark replied. 'Things have moved on rapidly since yesterday. This handbag crime has turned into a much more serious investigation.'

I had gone to the door with Mum and heard all of this. 'Gosh! Dead bodies all over the place?' I asked.

'No, nothing like that,' he replied. 'We did, however, find two more bags hidden in the woods. One of them has turned out to be quite remarkable.'

Katie, who had just joined us, asked, 'Wow, was one of them decorated with diamonds?'

'No, you are both wide of the mark,' Mark replied. 'This must be kept top secret,' he added. 'Is it possible for you to ask Johnny to come round? What I have to say affects him as well.'

Mum phoned Johnny's mum and Johnny soon appeared, panting hard. He had hurried over as fast as he could.

'Oh, hello, sir,' he said, on seeing Mark.

'I've just been explaining to Ben, Katie and their mum that the handbag crime has thrown up some interesting complications and these must be kept top secret. One of the handbags found later by our search team seemed rather heavier than expected. We could see no reason for this; it appeared to be a perfectly normal bag. So back at the station we had a closer look at it and got our forensic people to examine it. They X-rayed it and found a secret compartment in the bottom. Not only that, they saw it contained a small gun. A secret opening was found, cunningly disguised in the bag's lining. This compartment also contained a diary with some interesting coded messages in it. For example, the entry for April 12th: "Meeting X at station KC, platform 3 for drop at 18.33."

'We contacted the government's secret service, MI5, and showed them what we had found. They keep an eye on foreign spies, amongst other things. They are quite excited by our find. The gun, for example, is rather unusual, having been made in Slavodamia. This country, as you may know, is suspected of conducting sinister cybercrimes against the UK. They strongly suspect that the owner of the bag is a spy.

'The reason I'm telling you this is so that you avoid mentioning finding the handbags to anyone for the time being.'

'What about Colin Jenkins and the Rudley handbag he found?' Katie asked.

'We don't intend to take any further action on this, for the time being at least. I know this is unfortunate for the person who lost the bag, but we've decided it's best to let sleeping dogs lie in this instance. If we visit Colin's home and start questioning him about it, he's likely to guess there is more to it than simply someone losing a handbag whilst walking in the woods. Besides, if we park a police vehicle outside his house, the neighbours will wonder what's going on. Someone might even tip off the newspapers saying there could be a story here, and they might start asking awkward questions.

'We plan to quietly return the other handbags to their owners. We can ask them one at a time to attend the police station, telling them that their bag has been found, but not where. We've identified who owns most of them, as most contained items such as driving licences or credit cards. The thief only seems to have been interested in taking any cash found in them and removing mobile phones.

'Our main hope is that the owner of the handbag containing the gun and coded notebook doesn't suspect it has got into the hands of MI5. We hope she will think that the stolen bag has simply been thrown out and is now buried deep in a rubbish tip.'

'Have you found out who she is?' I asked.

'No,' Mark replied. 'There was nothing in the bag with her identity on it.'

'A shady lady,' Katie commented.

'Exactly,' Mark said. 'MI5 are obviously looking very thoroughly at the bag and its contents to try and work out who she might be.'

'And what about the handbag thief himself?' I asked.

'Well we're certainly keen to find him. We've actually found a car which matches Johnny's photo. The make and number plate are the same.'

'So you know who the thief is?' Johnny asked.

'Unfortunately not,' Mark replied. 'You see, although a car with that description and registration number does exist. It's been traced and belongs to an elderly lady living in the very far north of Scotland. The local police up there have looked into this matter and found that she only uses it to go to her local shops and otherwise keeps it locked in her garage. We're certain it was not the car Johnny photographed parked by the woods. The number plates fitted to the car you saw were obviously copies of those registered to the Scottish lady's car. Therefore, at present, we have no idea who the driver was. The only hope is that the man has not changed the plates back and can be caught still driving it. We've put out an alert for it to be stopped and the driver brought in for questioning.'

'Might they not inadvertently catch the Scottish lady out doing her shopping?' I asked.

'Well, we've thought of that and made sure this request does not apply in the north of Scotland,' Mark replied.

Sunday 20th February

Johnny came round this morning and asked if I'd heard any more about our mystery spy or the handbag thief. I told him I hadn't.

'As things seem to have gone quiet there, why don't we have another go at solving Mr Trinder's mystery coded message?' I suggested.

'Oh dear, such a lot seems to have happened since we last looked at it. I can't remember much about it,' was Johnny's reply. 'We could always drop the idea of solving it and have another game on my K-box!'

'Now then, Johnny,' I replied, 'are we detectives or aren't we? We might be onto finding treasure on some kind of desert island.'

'Yay, I'd forgotten about the treasure! Yes, we *are* detectives!' he replied. 'Okay, remind me where we had got to before we became involved in ladies' handbags.'

I reminded him that we had ruled out the use of a substitution type of code, one letter replacing another in order to make a message secret. We had decided that the code Mr Trinder had used was probably the rail fence type.

'If you remember, Johnny, you found a very strong hint that "rail" and "fence" were important in a separate note in the Jaguar owner's manual. This type of code hides a plain text message using a system for mixing up the letters.'

'Unscrambling them must be tricky,' Johnny remarked.

'Not really,' I said. 'Once you get the hang of the system, it's fairly straightforward, even if it is a bit time consuming. My codebook gives a simple example of how to put a message into a rail fence type code. The message to be coded in their example is: 'hiding a secret' and is based, as might be expected, on using a fence drawn on a piece of paper.'

I showed this example to Johnny. I've copied it down in my diary. In the example, alternate fence boards are coloured differently to help show how the coding is done.

The message to be coded is written along the fence, with one letter per fence board. Then alternate boards are slid out and placed to the right of the others. This gives the coded message.

Take a piece of fencing as shown below

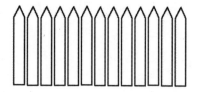

Write the message to be coded across it

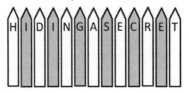

Select alternate upright boards and slide them out

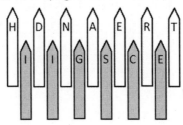

Place those slid out to the right of the others

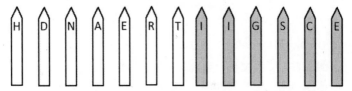

This gives the coded message as: HDNAERT.IIGSCE
Note: a full stop has been placed to show where the two sections were joined.

'To the unknowing reader the coded message, starting with the letters "HDNAERT", will appear to be gobbledegook!'

Johnny nodded and said, 'The example makes it look dead simple. Now I can see why full stops have been used in our coded message. They must show where the split up sections of text should be reunited side by side.'

'Good point,' I replied.

We looked again at the coded message which we had found in the owner's manual, in the old Jaguar. I've copied it out again below.

F S E E N H S Y L O S I H L O H Y E Z T B I A U 8 5 I E. O A
K P G I T B L N B N O Y U T T F Z I U E T 3 0 T S T. R F E I
W L M U I I E G T S G B H U I S R D S 5 3 H G S. W H 1 Y D
F A P N I B L I T E D A R 3 R F M T V L G E U B O. I I 0 A S
E C O T N A E N R A M S E Y D R I R E I D S T Y M. T N 0 R
O X T I F D L R A E N E U 2 A S O T A L N U O H C P. A I S
X E N E E T S S G S R Y E O D A P S O O O E L E O O C 1 0.
S T S T N C S E H M S E F A O S U I V A E N A T R A U R W
A 9. S I I E I H D P I E A I O N N H L H E S D T N H P C P D
N T 8

'I can see there are several sections of letters separated by full stops,' I said. 'We don't need to try and solve all of it at this stage. We need to check we are on the right lines first. Let's just try reversing the procedure used to create the coded message as shown in the example above, using just the first ten letters from each of the first two sections.'

Johnny agreed with this idea.

I then said to Johnny, 'I'm not going to draw bits of fencing, that would take too much time. I will simply place the letters from the first two sections of the coded message in two rows, with gaps between letters. Then we can slide the second row of letters up between alternate letters in the first row.'

I did this and obtained the following two lines of script.

Section 1 F S E E N H S Y L O

Section 2 O A K P G I T B L N

When alternate letters were merged together into one line the message looked like this:

FOSAEKEPNGHISTYBLLON

'Oh dear!' Johnny commented. 'It has a sort of ring of sense to it, but in fact it's meaningless.'

'We must have got something wrong somewhere,' I suggested. 'Still, we're probably on the right track. As you say, it has some words which almost have a meaning. "FOSAEK" could be "forsake" spelt slightly wrong, and "HISTY" could be read as "history". And remember, the rail fence system was strongly hinted at by Mr Trinder.

'I tell you what,' I added, 'when I was reading my book about this type of code, I remember it saying that some rail fence coded messages were more complicated than the one we have looked at. Instead of the plain text being split into two sections using every other letter, the coding split the plain text into three sections, taking letters in turn from each section. They show more clearly how this is done with an example.

'The example message they code is "Happy Birthday". The letters are written across the boards of a fence as in the earlier example. However, this time the boards are given three separate colours. This gives us three groups or sections of letters. The different coloured sections are then slid out and placed side by side as with our earlier rail fence coding. This gives a coded message which reads; H P I H Y. A Y R D. P B T A. To decode this message, the coding process is simply reversed.'

I attach a copy of their example in my diary below.

Message to be coded using every third letter,
giving three sections to be merged when decoding.

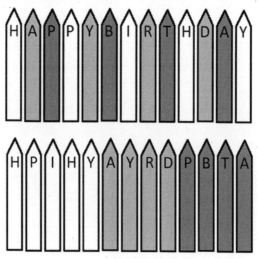

So our coded message is written out as:
HPIHY.AYRD.PBTA

'Perhaps we should try merging three sections of our coded message together,' Johnny suggested.

So, using the full stops in our coded message as separators, we produced the following set of letters, using the first ten letters from each of the first three sections of the coded message.

Section 1 F S E E N H S Y L O

Section 2 O A K P G I T B L N

Section 3 R F E I W L M U I I

The first two sections were the same as we had used before, but now we had a third section to merge, in between the earlier pairs. As we started this process, sensible words began to appear. The first was the word 'FOR'. It used the first letters from sections one, two and three. When the full merging process was completed it revealed the following message:

'FORSAFEKEEPINGWHILSTMYBULLIONI'.

By adding obvious spaces between words, the message became clear: 'FOR SAFE KEEPING WHILST MY BULLION I'.

'Woohoo!' Johnny shouted, jumping into the air. 'We've cracked it at last! And there *is* bullion involved, that must mean gold. How cool is that!'

'It must be worth a lot if we consider how much effort this Trinder bloke has gone to in coding his message,' I said. 'It must have taken him hours to work it all out. It's certainly taken us hours to get to this point.'

'What do we do next?' Johnny asked.

'Well, obviously one or both of us will have to tackle decoding the rest of the message,' I replied. 'It looks as if there is quite a prize at the end of it all. Mind you, if it is stolen treasure, we will have to hand it back to whoever it belongs to.'

'There could be a reward for it, even after all the years it must have been hidden,' Johnny suggested.

'We may well find someone else has already found it,' I replied. 'Still, at least we've had some fun busting Mr Trinder's code. We could complete decoding the rest of it if we each took a bit to work on. If you notice, there are nine sections to decode, each separated by a full stop. We have started on the first three sections. There are two more lots of three sections to go. If I finish the first and do the second lot, maybe you could tackle the last group of three sections. How about that?'

Johnny was happy with this suggestion, so we copied out the last three sections carefully, and he took them with him to work on when he went home.

Later on, I began work on decoding the rest of the

first three sections of the message. More sensible words began to appear, confirming that we were working along the right lines. It should have been apparent to me earlier that Mr Trinder had not been pairing just two sections of his message at a time. This would have only used up the first eight sections of his message. As there were nine sections in total spit up by full stops, this would have left one section that had nothing to be paired with.

By bedtime I had nearly finished merging the first three sections. I decided I would finish it tomorrow.

Monday 21st February

Johnny rang up and told me he had not finished decoding his bit of the message, as he'd had homework to do. However, he would come round tomorrow evening after school and, all being well, we could put our separate pieces of message together then. This suited me as I had not had time to finish deciphering the first three sections, let alone the next three I had agreed to work on. I had quite a bit of English homework to finish, which took priority as Mrs Standish, the English teacher, wanted it in tomorrow. I also needed to take Millie and Chippy out for some exercise.

Tuesday 22nd February

Much the same as yesterday. Had homework to do, maths this time. So I've not done any more work on decoding Mr Trinder's message.

I also had a phone call from Mark Riley, our detective friend. He said they had made good progress with finding the handbag snatcher and could he pop in to see us tomorrow evening? He suggested Johnny would also be interested, so would I ask him if he could come round too?

I rang Johnny and he said of course he would be able to come. He couldn't wait to see what the police had turned up. In fact, he said, 'Wickedly wild wallabies won't keep me away!'

He likes to make dramatic little statements, stringing together words beginning with the same first letter. I think this is called alliteration. Mrs Standish was telling us about this last week, which shows I do listen to some of what she says. However, my mind does sometimes wander, especially when I'm thinking about a mystery or crime we have been working on.

Johnny likes to sit and watch the trains going past! He can see them out of his classroom window. Despite this he still usually gets quite good marks in most subjects, although his school report on spelling usually says, 'Could do better,' or so he tells me. Fortunately, computers these days can do a spellcheck and suggest the correct spelling if you make a mistake. Not that this is always helpful. Firstly, we're not allowed to take computers into class. Secondly, some words which sound the same are spelt differently and have different meanings. 'PLANE' and 'PLAIN' are an example. I get mixed up with these, although PLANE is often used as a shortened version of aeroplane and the other spelling means 'not fancy'. As an example, we might say: 'They had a PLAIN green carpet'.

I don't know why I put this in my diary. Still, now I have, I am not going to cross it out!

Wednesday 23rd February

Mark Riley came round this evening. Johnny and I were excited to see what he had to say. Katie was also keen to see if the handbag thief had been found.

Before Mark arrived, Johnny came up to my bedroom to discuss what progress we had made with deciphering the coded message. We also wondered if we should mention it to Mark when he came. But we decided to work out what it said first. Then we could let him in on our secret, if it proved important.

When Mark arrived, Mum invited him into our lounge and offered him a cup of tea. As he was not officially on duty he accepted and she fetched him his tea and a few biscuits.

When we were all seated, Mark said, 'Well now, thanks to Johnny's photo of the car, plus a local estate agent, we have managed to catch the handbag snatcher.'

Good news, I thought, *but what could an estate agency have to do with the case? Surely they just sell houses.*

Mark explained, 'You see, when estate agency sales staff are out showing people round houses, the office manager likes to keep a track of where they are. He sometimes has a new customer arrive wanting to be shown round a certain house. By knowing where each of his sales team is, he may be able to slot the new customer into one of their planned routes. Also, it's important to be able to locate his staff quickly in case, as has happened, one goes missing. If they don't turn up for their next appointment the question arises, where are they? They may have been taken ill or had an accident. The manager told me there was a case recently when one of his staff fell down some stairs after his customer had left. He broke a leg and banged his head. We were able to locate him when his wife phoned in asking why he hadn't got home from work. He had told her he wouldn't be late. He's okay now, but being able to send someone to find him and get him to hospital quickly made a big difference. He made a speedy recovery.

'To do all this, the estate agency manager has provided each member of his sales team with a mobile phone which has a location tracking app. He can therefore see where they are at any one time. He can do this by looking at a map on his office computer. Each member of staff appears as a small individual circle on the map, indicating their location at that moment. This is where the stolen handbag case comes in.

'A female member of the sales team had just finished her lunch break. As she was leaving a sandwich bar, a man on a bike cycled past and grabbed her bag. The thief was obviously using the same method for stealing bags as described by our earlier victims.

'The lady concerned contacted the estate agency manager and reported the theft of her bag and the mobile which was in it. By looking on his computer he could see where the phone was being taken. At first, he could see it was on the move, travelling northwards along various local streets. After a while it stopped moving and he was able to pick out where it had got to. It was not possible to pinpoint exactly which house it had been taken into, but he was able to pin it down to within three or four neighbouring houses.

'He phoned us with this information. I sent one of my officers to the approximate location and he spotted the car Johnny had photographed near the woods. It was parked outside one of the houses. It had a different number plate, but there were two stickers on the front windscreen which matched exactly with those seen on the car Johnny photographed. We obtained a search warrant to search the house concerned. The man who opened the door denied knowing anything about the stolen handbag. But the search warrant overrode the man's objections and the ensuing search soon revealed the location of the bag. It was found among several others which he must have also stolen. The mobile phone was still in it, giving its location.'

'Wow! That was fortunate,' Katie said.

'It's a wonder he hadn't got rid of the phone; he might have smashed it with a hammer and put it in a local rubbish bin,' I suggested.

'He probably would have in the normal way of things,' Mark replied. 'However, the bag in question was unusual. It was a handmade patchwork one made by the estate agent sales lady's aunt. Her aunt likes making quilts and other things. She had given her niece a patchwork handbag as a birthday present. It has several unusual features, including a concealed pocket. The mobile phone was in this pocket, which has every appearance of being just another patch. Our bag-snatching thief had found the money in the bag, but not realised it also contained a mobile phone. So in this case we were somewhat lucky, as it enabled us to track down our culprit.'

'I should think the lady who had her unusual bag found will be very pleased to get it back,' Mum commented.

'Yes,' Mark replied. 'But at present we need it as evidence. It will naturally go back to its owner in due course.'

'Talking of secret handbag pockets,' Johnny asked, 'is there any news about the other bag, the one which had a concealed compartment containing a gun?

'Ah!' Mark replied. 'We have heard practically nothing from MI5 and don't expect to hear much more any time soon. The little bit of information we have gleaned indicates they still don't know who the owner is.

'However,' he added, 'in the meantime, none of us know anything about this, do we?' He rubbed the side of his nose meaningfully.

'Ah yes! It's all TOP SECRET,' Johnny replied, emphasising the last two words.

'That's right,' Mark replied.

After Mark had gone, Johnny and I decided we would leave trying to join up our separate bits of decoded message until tomorrow after school. I had yet to finish sorting out the final three sections, and Johnny was in a similar position with the sections he was working on. We agreed to try and finish our work on this tonight and have it ready for tomorrow.

So Johnny set off home and I went back to my bedroom.

Thursday 24th February

After school Johnny came round with his decoded portion of the message. I had finished decoding my bits, and when joined up, with spacings put in between the recognisable words and some punctuation added, the message read as follows:

'FOR SAFE KEEPING, WHILST MY BULLION IS BEING HOTLY SOUGHT BY THE FUZZ, IT IS BURIED AT SU 358035. THIS GETS WITHIN 100 YARDS OF EXACT POINT. FIND BALLERINA TREE AND MEASURE 23 YARDS FROM IT, TRAVELLING DUE SOUTH BY COMPASS. IT IS SIXTEEN INCHES DEEP. THIS MESSAGE IS FOR ANYONE, SHOULD I HAVE PASSED ON TO ANOTHER PLACE UP OR DOWN. CAT 1980.'

'Woohoo! Buried treasure!' Johnny cried.

'Certainly looks like it,' I agreed.

'Where is SU358035 and what about the ballerina tree?' Johnny asked.

'Sounds like another coded message,' I suggested.

'Katie might know,' Johnny replied hopefully.

We found Katie in her bedroom talking to a friend on her mobile. I showed her our decoded message.

'I have to go now, Poppy,' she said into her phone. 'Something important has just cropped up!'

On reading the message, Katie exclaimed. 'Yay! This is amazing, you appear to have a treasure hunt on your hands!'

'Yes, but where is SU358035, and do you know anything about ballerina trees?' I asked.

'Well, first things first,' she replied. 'The SU number looks like an Ordnance Survey grid reference. We have been studying maps in geography class at school. Using the Ordnance Survey, or OS maps, any point within England, Scotland and Wales can be pinpointed using a grid reference. First of all, Britain is divided into squares, each labelled using two letters, such as NY and TQ. Your reference starts with the letters SU.'

She typed a few instructions into her laptop and said, 'Ah yes! I have found your area. It lies in Hampshire just north of the Isle of Wight. The Isle of Wight is SZ, your area SU is on the mainland just to the north of this. The numbers 358035, which follow SU, show a point within this area to within 100 metres. If you had a map with area SU on it, you could fairly accurately find the spot you're both looking for.'

'Unfortunately I don't have such a map,' I pointed out.

'Yes, but if you did, you could look up the position of SU358035 by using the first three numbers: 358 to find where to look by going left to right on the map, and the next three going bottom to top. To remember, remember this: "In through the door and then up the stairs". All OS maps are numbered along the margins to help you find a location in this way.'

'Okay,' I replied. 'So I now need an OS map for the area SU.'

'Yes!' Katie replied. 'Now I must go and do some homework.'

Once we were back in my room, Johnny asked me, 'Did all that make sense to you?'

'No,' I replied truthfully. 'But it looks like we need an Ordnance Survey map of an area just north of the Isle of Wight. I wonder if Uncle David might have one. He tends to collect old maps.'

'And what about ballerina trees?' Johnny said. 'Katie didn't say anything about those.'

'Yes,' I replied. 'I think she forgot. I will look on the Internet and see what it has to tell us about them.'

It soon emerged that there are two very different kinds of ballerina tree. Firstly, there is a variety of apple tree which has this name. And secondly one or two old woodland trees have, over the years, become misshapen and come to look a bit like posing ballet dancers.

Johnny was quite pleased with the idea of apple trees and said, 'Well at least we won't get hungry on our treasure hunt!'

'You'll be lucky,' I replied, 'it's February, rather late for apple picking.'

'Or too early,' he quipped.

We left any further discussion on what the decoded message had told us for another day.

Friday 25ᵗʰ February

After I'd had my tea, I phoned Uncle David and asked him if he had an Ordnance Survey map with the area just north of the Isle of Wight on it.

'It should have grid references starting with "SU" on it,' I told him.

He looked in his map collection and said, 'You're in luck; I have an OS Landranger map of the Isle of Wight which also covers an area of mainland England just to the north of the island. What is the actual grid reference you have?'

I told him and he said, 'Now then, hold on, let me look it up.'

After a moment he came back to me and said he had found the location. 'It's in the New Forest.'

'Dead cool!' I replied.

'Are you on a treasure hunt or something?' he jokingly asked.

'Well, yes, as a matter of fact, we are!' I replied.

I explained what we had found so far. He was well impressed.

'Golly! Buried treasure, I think this might call for some help from my metal detector,' he suggested.

'Yes,' I replied, 'the one we used to hunt for Lady Brigg's valuable ring a month or so ago.'

'That's the one,' he replied.

To cut a long story short, it has been arranged that

Auntie Maudie will take us all to the New Forest in her new camper van. She had been looking for an excuse to go on a trip in it. This seemed the perfect opportunity to try it out. We plan to go there a week on Saturday. We're hoping to set off early in the morning, taking a picnic with us. Her camper van has a cooker hotplate in it, so lots of hot drinks can be brewed up, which will please Auntie, Mum and Gran. It also has a fridge to put some cans of ginger beer in, which will please Johnny, Katie and myself. Also there will be a can or two of lager for Uncle David!

I checked to see if Johnny could come.

'You bet I'll come,' Johnny squawked. 'Treasure hunting sounds well good. Do you think we can keep what we find?'

I told him we had better inform the police if we found anything valuable.

'You must remember, it was stolen by Charlie Trinder. He was a criminal and his loot is stolen property. I expect the owners will want it back even though it was stolen forty or more years ago.'

'There might still be a reward for anyone finding it!' Johnny suggested hopefully.

'In the meantime we don't know whether we *will* find anything. Let's wait and see if there is anything still buried there before we start thinking about rewards,' I told him.

'Yes, I suppose you're right,' Johnny said. 'But don't forget we must take the Jaguar owner's manual with us. It has that roughly drawn map on one of the pages. This might help us find the exact location.'

I agreed.

'Firstly we have to find the ballerina tree,' Johnny reminded me. 'I wonder what sort it is?'

'Apple or weirdly shaped,' I replied. 'And we need to take a long tape measure and compass with us to help find the spot where the so-called treasure was buried. Uncle David has agreed to take his metal detector, which should help us find the exact location.'

Saturday 26th February

Johnny came round first thing. We dug out the Jag's owner's manual, which had once belonged to Charlie Trinder. The sketch map seemed to show plenty of trees, a pond and some open space.

'This must be somewhere in the New Forest,' I said to Johnny. 'If Auntie Maudie can drive us close to where Uncle David's map shows the place to be, this map could well be key to locating the treasure. However, remember, as it was drawn over forty years ago, things may have changed in this area since then. For example, some of the trees may have been cut down or new ones planted.'

'Also the ballerina tree we are looking for may have been struck by lightning and just be a dead stump now,' Johnny added pessimistically.

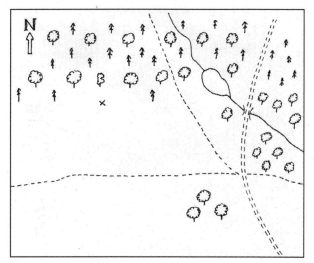

Johnny and I opened the Jag's owner's manual at the page where the map had been drawn. It showed a lot of features such as footpaths, a pond, a stream and, of course, plenty of trees. We decided to show it to Uncle David, so he knew what we were looking for when we got to the New Forest. We also noticed a single cross marked and wondered if this might indicate where the treasure had been buried.

Fortunately, Uncle David was home when we arrived at his and Gran's house. Gran invited us in and gave us some ginger beer, which she keeps in a cupboard for young visitors. Gran was delighted to see Millie and Chippy, who had come with us. She found them a few treats and showed them her garden. Millie had a good sniff around and Chippy checked her bird table for more eats!

Johnny and I found Uncle David in his workshop and showed him the sketch map. He decided to make a photocopy of it.

'I will compare this with my OS map and see if it matches the map's details for the grid reference you gave me,' he told us. 'But that will have to wait, as I have a friend coming round later and I'm presently in the middle of preparing some drawings for him.'

We thanked Gran for the drinks and made our way back to our homes, as it was almost lunchtime.

*

This afternoon Mum took me and Katie shopping. She said I needed new socks and Katie fancied some glittery lipstick. All very exciting! ☹

However, soon after we had returned home, Auntie Maudie called and asked if we would like to go for a picnic tomorrow in Richmond Park. We could follow this by having a walk to see the deer. We of course said it would be great. 'Can we take Millie?' Katie asked.

Auntie Maudie replied, 'Of course Millie can come. She can run free in the park. Chippy might also like to come. There are lots of old oak trees for him to explore. He might even find a few grubs and other creepy crawlies to munch, although I admit most are likely to be hiding until it's a warmer time of year.'

I rang Johnny to see if he would like to join us, but he said that his cousin Cedric and family were visiting, so he couldn't come, worse luck.

Sunday 27th February

As planned, Auntie Maudie and Gran picked us up mid-morning in her camper van, Connie, and drove us to Richmond Park. This is a large Royal Park on the edge of London. When we arrived, we had our sandwiches and drinks. Chippy had some cake crumbs I had brought for him and Millie had a drink of water in her bowl. Not to be left out on the food front, Katie had brought a dog biscuit for Millie. We then set off for a walk around the park. There was a notice board instructing people to respect the deer and not get too close.

Auntie Maudie reminded us that the deer were, after all, wild animals.

She told us, 'The stags, or male deer, are the most dangerous. They grow large antlers and in the autumn fight each other to gain supremacy. They do this by charging at each other and locking antlers. The strongest push the weaker ones around and try and inflict injuries on them. Generally, the weaker stags will back off and group together, waiting to fight another day, usually the following autumn. The autumn fighting period is called the rut.'

We came across a large number of deer. They were herded together in a group, grazing on the grass quietly. This herd consisted mainly of hinds or female deer, with a few youngsters and one large stag. Although she was off the lead, Millie was very well behaved and made no attempt to get close to them. Chippy, on the other hand, decided to inspect them close up and landed on one. They were obviously used to seeing small birds and took no notice of him.

As it was now late February, the rut period was well over and we saw no stags fighting. We did, however, come across a lone stag. He was a magnificent creature with very large antlers. Although we were quite a distance away, he gave us a hard look. I took a photo of him with the zoom setting on my camera. Millie may have caused him to look hard-faced. Apparently, some dog owners are stupid and allow their dogs to chase the deer. They then wonder why they end up with huge veterinary bills, or worse. Stags can do serious damage to a dog using its sharply pointed antlers. Even humans who get too close can end up in hospital, unless they are very good at climbing a handy tree!

After walking a fair distance further on, we came across a large fenced-off area. We found a gate into it. There was a notice next to it which told us that this was the Isabella Plantation. It also informed us that it had been a very boggy area and of little value for grazing animals like cattle and deer. So around two hundred years ago, it had been fenced off and planted with trees and shrubs to make an interesting garden area. The fencing was needed to keep out the deer and cattle grazing in the park. The last thing they wanted was livestock munching all the newly planted shrubs and trees. The wettest areas had been used to create several large ponds.

We entered through the gate. A further notice said, 'Dogs must be kept on a lead'. We did as we were told. Chippy, of course, flew in over the gate and found a nice tree to settle in. It being wintertime, most of the trees were bare of any leaves. However, some of the shrubby plants, like rhododendrons, had leaves so there was plenty of greenery, but no flowers. It was pleasant to wander round, with lots of streams and ponds with ducks in them. What I liked best were the old, hollow-trunked oak trees. Some had become bent and twisted with age and were now quite distorted. One in particular looked to me like a pot-bellied old man! Another tree had been felled, and it was fun to walk along its trunk just a few feet above the ground. It was a bit like tightrope walking. I bet Johnny would have enjoyed this if he had been with us.

When we got back to Connie, I wonder if you can guess what the first thing Mum and Auntie Maudie did? They did what they always do after an outing: they put the kettle on to make a cup of tea!

Friday 4th March

I have been busy all this week with school and homework. However, I have been excitedly looking forward to tomorrow's trip to the New Forest and our planned treasure hunt. I know Johnny has been excited by this prospect. He has sent me text messages nearly every day telling me there are only however many days until Saturday! He popped round this evening to see if he should bring some sandwiches.

Saturday 5th March

As planned, Auntie Maudie and Uncle David called for Katie, Mum and me in camper van Connie at eight o'clock. Gran had decided to do some shopping so was not joining us this time. Johnny rushed up just in time, a few minutes after eight, all out of breath.

'We were about to set off without you!' I told him. 'Only joking,' I added, 'but if you had been another five minutes later, we would have had to come looking for you!'

The drive to the New Forest was uneventful and we arrived well before ten o'clock. We pulled into a car park near a stream and had the usual cups of tea for Mum and Auntie Maudie and ginger beer for us kids and Uncle David. Then we consulted our maps of the area, including the sketch map from the Jaguar's owner's manual. Uncle David had got hold of a large-scale map of the part of the New Forest that included the grid reference we had found.

'I have been studying the location where the loot is supposed to be buried,' Uncle David told us. 'However, I must say it does not show any similar landmarks to those on the sketch map. For example, there is no pond or stream nearby, nor is there a drivable track near the site.'

'Oh dear!' Johnny commented, 'Perhaps the whole thing is a hoax!'

'So much for your bullion,' Katie remarked, rather

sarcastically.

'Hold on a minute,' Uncle David cried, waving his OS map about. 'Before you write the whole thing off, I think I may have spotted what has happened here. I noticed this before we set out, so I looked for an area on my map which did match up with the sketch map and, surprise, I found one that *did* match. I think your Mr T was not terribly good at looking up grid references. If I take his 358035 and reverse his last three and five, it pinpoints a place which does make sense.

'I suggest we drive there first and see if we can find the ballerina tree or what remains of it. And by the way, I have done a bit of research on ballerina trees. We do not need to look for an apple tree; the ballerina variety only became available fifteen years ago. It was not around when Mr Trinder was burying his treasure.'

'So we're just looking for a tree shaped like a ballet dancer,' I replied.

'Exactly,' Uncle David agreed.

'Okay,' Auntie Maudie said. 'Give me instructions on how to find this magic location and I will drive us there. Mind, I shall be cross if you land Connie in a bog,' she added.

The track leading to our so-called magic area proved to be quite good and Auntie Maudie parked just before the bridge which crossed the stream, as shown on the sketch map.

Uncle David had a rucksack which contained a

collapsible army spade, his metal detector and a one hundred metre surveyors' tape measure. He had also brought a garden trowel.

I had brought my compass.

Millie was rather excited. She had seen Uncle David's metal detector before and knew this could mean hole digging. She considers hole digging to be one of her specialities! We set off in a westerly direction to start with, Chippy happily flying above us. We crossed a footpath which was running in a north-westerly direction. This was shown on the sketch map. We began to feel we were in the right location and that perhaps not too much had altered since the sketch map had been drawn. We then turned slightly to the north. So far, we had been crossing a fairly large expanse of rough grassland, with a few New Forest ponies grazing peacefully on it.

As shown on the sketch map, there were trees to the north of us. We were keeping an eye out for any tree which might look like a ballerina. We were not sure what to look for. Ballerinas take on all sorts of poses when dancing. Would the tree have two raised arm-like branches forming a loop, or what?

Katie spotted it first. 'Look,' she shouted, 'over there, there's a tree that does look like a ballerina holding a kind of pose.'

Auntie Maudie, who is keen on ballet, agreed. 'I

think they call that ballet position the *penché*,' she said.

Johnny ran over to the tree, so I snapped a photo of him standing by it. This would make a useful record; with Johnny next to it, we would get an idea of how tall it was. It did not seem large as trees go. Johnny looked as if he was thinking about climbing it!

The rest of us caught up with him soon afterwards.

'Right, who has a compass?' Uncle David asked, taking the surveyors' tape measure out of his rucksack. I found my compass and looked to see where due south was.

'Okay, Johnny,' Uncle David said, 'you hold this end of the tape against the tree here and I will measure twenty-three yards in a roughly southerly direction. Then if Ben stands next to you he can signal to me which way to move to be due south of the tree.'

Fortunately, Uncle David's tape measure had measurements in metres on one side and yards and inches on the other, so measuring twenty-three yards was no problem. Uncle David gave the thumbs up when he had reached the required distance.

'Left a bit,' I shouted and Uncle David moved a bit to the right!

He had moved to *his* left, but as he was facing us it was to *our* right!

'No! The other way,' I shouted.

'Right, quite a lot,' Johnny shouted.

'Make up your minds, you two,' Uncle David shouted back.

Auntie Maudie thought this was great fun and shouted, 'Sort yourself out, David, they were right first time. You don't know your left from your right!'

Eventually, after a bit of backchat between Auntie Maudie, Uncle David and us boys, Uncle David found the exact location and dropped his rucksack on it.

Chippy meanwhile had perched himself in the tree and sat there watching what was going on. He made some happy chirpings. Perhaps it was his way of showing amusement.

Next, Uncle David took out his metal detector and ran it over the area. It made a very loud whistling sound. He looked very pleased with himself. 'Found it in one,' he said as we came up to him.

'It's very loud,' I commented.

'Bit too loud if you ask me,' he replied.

'You don't think it found the spade in your rucksack, do you?' I asked.

'Oh! I never thought of that,' Uncle replied grinning. 'How silly, yes of course it's the spade in my bag!'

So we moved the rucksack well out of the way and Johnny found a stick and we pushed into the ground to mark where it had been. We hoped we would now find the treasure below the stick or at least close by.

'Okay, I'll start searching again,' Uncle David said, beginning for a second time to hunt for the treasure.

'Will your detector find gold?' Johnny asked. 'We know it can detect old rusty nails from your earlier searches, but can it locate gold?'

'No problem,' Uncle David replied. 'It's set up to find all types of metal including gold. Besides, if you remember, it helped locate a gold ring not very long ago.'

'We're told the booty is buried eighteen inches deep,' I reminded him. 'Do you think you can find it down there?'

'Yes, should be a piece of cake,' he replied.

'Chippy will be pleased if you find some cake!' Auntie Maudie quipped. She had just joined us in our search. 'Mind, if it's forty years old, I don't think it will taste very nice!'

'Okay, that's enough humour for now,' Uncle David replied, 'let's see what we can find.'

He continued searching the area, but his metal detector remained completely silent. By the time he had swept an area of about three metres around the stick, we were beginning to doubt there was anything to find. Maybe someone had already found it, or perhaps it had all been a joke on Mr Trinder's part. This was very dispiriting.

'Do you think we've found the wrong tree?' Johnny asked.

'Well this one does look like a ballerina,' Katie told him. 'There cannot be too many that look like that in this woodland, or even in the whole of Britain.'

'Perhaps the twenty-three yards Mr T measured was just paced out,' I wondered.

'It seems a fairly definite value,' Uncle David replied. 'Why twenty-three and not twenty or twenty-five? Still, I will scan the ground walking back towards the tree, in case it wasn't an accurate measurement.' He did this and found one old horseshoe, but no treasure.

'This is rather disappointing. Try scanning the ground, walking further away from the tree,' Katie suggested.

Uncle David did this, but still nothing set his metal detector squealing.

'Well, whilst you carry on looking for this supposed buried treasure, I am going back to Connie to fetch a rug and our lunch,' Auntie Maudie told us.

'I'll come with you,' Mum added.

Whilst they set off, we all sat down to think what we should do next, if anything.

I said, 'I think we must have found the right tree. As Katie says, there cannot be many trees that look like ballerinas. This must be the right one. It also fits in with the other features shown on the map, the pond, the stream and the footpaths.'

'I agree,' Uncle David replied. 'Is it just one more problem Mr T has set us? He got his grid reference muddled, could he have got the twenty-three yards measurement wrong?'

Johnny replied, 'Well, you have searched shorter and longer distances from the tree and found nothing, so that can't be the problem.'

By this time Mum and Auntie Maudie arrived

with the rug and our picnic, so we all sat down for lunch.

Chippy, of course, joined us and began looking for some nibbles! Millie on the other hand was good and didn't make any attempt at begging for food.

We discussed our lack of success with Mum and Auntie Maudie. Uncle David's searches had, to say the least, been very disappointing.

After the lunch had been packed away, Uncle David suddenly stood up and clasped his hands over his head. 'I know what the problem is!' he declared.

'Oh yes?' Auntie Maudie remarked sceptically. 'Don't tell me, you forgot your bicycle clips!'

'Don't be silly, Maudie! It's nothing like that. The problem is that magnetic north is not in a constantly fixed position. Over time it moves. From our position in Britain it has been moving from west to east bit by bit every year. In fact, this movement has speeded up over the last thirty to forty years. I remember reading an article about it recently, in a science magazine we have at work.'

Uncle David is a bit of a boffin, which means he knows about a lot of scientific stuff like magnetism, electricity, atomic energy and so on.

'When your Mr T measured out this spot in about 1980, magnetic north by his compass would have been quite a bit further to the west than it is now,'

Uncle David told us. 'The magnetic north pole was in Canada then, many miles west of the true north pole. It is now in the Arctic Ocean, almost in line with the true north pole. By the same token, the south pole pointer on his compass would have pointed a lot further east then compared with today.'

'Surely this won't have affected our measurements by much, will it?' I asked. Uncle David took out a notebook and drew a picture of a compass and showed how much the needle direction had changed since 1980. I have tidied his drawing up for my diary!

COMPASS NORTH

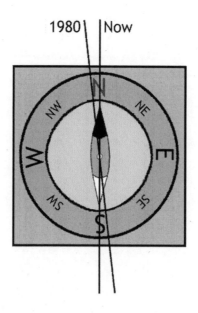

He then said to me, 'Go and stand by the ballerina tree again with your compass. Check that where we put that stick in the ground still lines up with your compass south. If it's okay, give me a thumbs up. Then using my diagram, line me up with where it would have been back in 1980. You can line me up using hand signals like this…' He showed me what he meant. 'Hopefully this time we will find where Mr T buried his gold.'

'Before I go back to the ballerina tree,' I said, 'can you explain why magnetic north is moving?'

'It's all to do with the liquid molten magma which lies deep below the earth's crust,' Uncle explained. 'The molten material acts as a giant magnet, and as it very slowly swirls around deep down, magnetic north shifts with it.'

'Don't you think you ought to get on with searching for this treasure, instead of standing here discussing nuclear physics?' Auntie Maudie suggested.

'Well, nuclear physics *has* actually got a bit to do with keeping the earth's magma molten, but our present problem is mainly about shifting magnetism,' Uncle David told her curtly.

(Note: Uncle David and Auntie Maudie are brother and sister and we often notice a bit of sibling rivalry between them!)

Anyway, after this little exchange, I went back to

the ballerina tree and, using my compass again, found our stick *was* still in line with magnetic south as shown on my compass. So I gave Uncle David a thumbs up. Then, using his diagram, I lined him up with where he reckoned magnetic south would have been back in 1980.

The new position was about five metres to the east of the stick. This was only a little outside the area Uncle David had searched earlier. He searched again in this new location, and we heard his metal detector begin to signal. It was not very loud, but nevertheless it was a definite squeal.

'Keep your fingers crossed this time,' Uncle David told us, and assembling his collapsible army spade, he began to dig. First he removed a circular patch of turf and laid it to one side. Then out came the topsoil layer, which he placed on a plastic sheet he had brought with him for this purpose.

'It keeps the soil off the grass and helps us when we put it back in the hole later,' he explained. 'Otherwise it can make the surrounding grass look messy.'

'I can tell you've done this sort of thing before,' Katie commented.

'Well, I am what you call a part-time detectorist, and we hunters of buried treasure like to leave a site as we found it, when digging for buried bits of history.'

'Like the odd nail?' Johnny commented cheekily.

Milly had been looking excitedly at the developing hole, so we let her do a bit of digging. She was not quite as tidy as Uncle David and sent soil flying all over the place!

She unearthed an object at about fourteen inches down. It turned out to be an old leather glove; perhaps it had been left there by Mr T?

I then did a bit of digging myself and very soon struck something soft. It was the other leather glove!

Johnny then had a turn. He struck something hard. Uncle David brought out a small trowel and handed it to him.

'Use this and go carefully now. Try and dig around whatever it is down there so we can see how large it is,' he told him.

So he worked his way around what appeared to be a box. It was disappointingly small, only about twelve centimetres across. Having uncovered the top of it, he dug around it. It was stuck tightly in the ground, and Johnny could not shift it. Uncle David took over again and soon had the soil round the hard object loosened up enough to prise the whole thing out of the ground. It was indeed a small box.

Katie, who had been waiting to see what we had found, told us, 'Whilst you were all busy digging the hole, I don't know if you noticed, but a woman came across the field with her dog. She stopped fairly close by and stared at us for quite a time. I think she was curious to see what we were up to.'

'She might have thought we were digging up plants,' Uncle David suggested. 'People are not allowed to do that in National Parks.'

'She's gone now. Let's hope she doesn't report us to the local park wardens,' Katie replied.

'I think we should hide our find in my rucksack, then fill in our hole as neatly as we can and then make a rapid exit,' Uncle David suggested.

So he placed the rather soil-covered box in his rucksack, together with the two old gloves. Then he carefully replaced the subsoil, followed by the upper soil layers and finally the turf. It looked quite a tidy repair job. The soil had bulked up pretty well, so there was no obvious hollow at the surface even though the box was no longer present. There was still a bit of fine soil round where the pit had been, thanks mainly to Millie. However, Uncle David reckoned that next time it rained, this would wash down through the turf, making where we had just dug practically invisible. He folded up his spade and popped this together with his tape measure in his rucksack. He had to carry the metal detector separately as there was now no room for it in his bag.

We got back to Connie uneventfully and quickly set off in case any park wardens had been alerted to our goings-on. After about ten miles we pulled into a lay-by for Mum and Auntie Maudie to have a cuppa! Millie was given some water and us kids had some more ginger beer whilst Uncle David was presented with a can of lager. Mum told him he deserved it after his success in locating the buried box. Chippy chirped, making his presence known, and was found some of his favourite cake crumbs.

Johnny asked Uncle David if we could examine the box we had found. But Uncle David replied that we should wait until we got back home, as it had rather a thick coating of soil on it.

'We don't want to upset Connie, or your Auntie Maudie for that matter, by getting mud all over these clean carpets,' he told Johnny. 'I will say one thing, though: if this box is supposed to contain stolen bullion, it seems to be very light in weight. Gold is weighty stuff. If there was gold in this box, I would expect it to feel much heavier.'

'Perhaps it contains diamonds or other valuable gems,' Katie suggested hopefully.

'Yes, maybe,' uncle replied.

'Let's hope Katie's right,' Johnny remarked. 'Otherwise all that time we spent breaking the coded message will have been a complete waste. Just think, we could have been playing computer games!'

'Really, Johnny!' Katie told him. 'You will end up with square eyes and have to wear thick-lensed glasses before you reach your teens if you're not careful. I am sure the code breaking was much better for you than time spent playing silly games!'

'They are *not* silly,' Johnny groaned, 'they allow us to relax after lots of brain-busting schoolwork.'

'Now then, children,' Uncle David interrupted. 'Whatever's in the box, it was not a waste of time. We succeeded in finding what was buried at the spot marked 'X' on the Trinder map. And you now know all about the movement of magnetic north. Let's see what we have found before complaining that it's been a wild goose chase.'

When we got to Gran and Uncle David's house, we were invited in for a latish dinner. Whilst Gran and Mum were getting the meal ready, Uncle David suggested we go into his workshop to look at the box and see what it contained.

We were excited to see what we had found. Was it a bag of gold coins or perhaps a few diamonds?

First of all, Uncle David put some newspaper over part of his bench, and then he removed the rather soil-coated box from his rucksack and placed it on the paper. After he had scraped off most of the soil with a decorator's scraper, we could see it was covered with what Uncle David told us was oilcloth. It had been neatly stitched at the seams to fit the box exactly.

'I expect this was to keep the box watertight,' Uncle David told us. 'I must carefully remove it with a sharp knife.'

This he did, exposing a rather rusty old biscuit tin. It still had some of the manufacturer's pattern on it. The oilcloth had done quite a good job of keeping it dry.

'This is dead cool,' Johnny exclaimed. 'I wonder what we will find?'

'We'll soon find out if I can prise this lid off,' Uncle David replied. 'After all the years it's been in the ground, it's become rusted on.'

He pulled at it and struggled with it, but the lid would not budge. After a while he said, 'I know, I'll try spraying round under the lid with some rust-releasing oil.'

This he did, then pulled some more, getting his hands covered in rusty oil.

At this point, Auntie Maudie popped her head around the door and told us dinner was ready.

'Wash your hands and come and get it,' she told us.

'The top may loosen up if we leave the oil to seep in,' Uncle David told us. So we left the tin to be opened later.

After dinner we returned with Uncle David to his workshop. The lid came off the tin fairly easily, having sat soaking up the oil.

'So now is the moment of truth!' Katie said rather dramatically.

With bated breath, we waited to see what was in the tin. First there was a layer of newspaper and then wrapped in tissue paper was a round cylinder-shaped object.

Uncle carefully lifted it out and took off the tissue paper covering. The cylinder turned out to be a glass jar with a screw-top lid. We could see a roll of paper inside.

'You'd better open this jar, Johnny,' he said, 'as you found the owner's manual in Mr T's Jaguar, which led us to this find.'

Johnny took the jar. The lid unscrewed fairly easily and Johnny gently removed the rolled-up paper. As it came out there was a rattle of keys. Two keys on a keyring fell out; they had been hidden between the folds of paper.

We watched him unfold the paper. 'Oh no, not more codes!' he muttered, passing the paper to me and Katie. There was a message in plain English first, followed by a jumble of unintelligible numbers.

I read out the message so we could all digest its content. It said:

'Anyone finding this will perhaps be disappointed not to find what they were looking for.'

'That's an understatement,' Uncle David muttered.

It continued: 'I have decided that anyone with a metal detector out hunting coins, etcetera, could stumble across my booty by chance. So rather than risk placing it here I have decided it should be hidden in a safer place. So chapter two of this affair will be one of the keys to locating the booty; the others are enclosed.'

'These two metal keys must be the "others" he mentions,' Johnny suggested.

'Yes, but goodness knows what the other one, the third key, is,' I said.

'It must be the key to solving the coded message he has enclosed,' Katie reckoned.

The jumbled numbers were:

277 447 77 528 415 157 100 346 16 343 106 105 411 232 9 511 333 21 33 380 415 214 207 83 404 430 102 65 432 148 271 552 27 210 60 121 556 397 675 67 41 626 99 375 372 223 136 207 303 212 552 386 88 405 197 76 84 26 234 273 461 129 139 245 108 28 565 211 107 363 261 72 98 281 9 157 579 633 248 104 568 84 46 481 200 546 170 505 473 26 180 270 78 160 491 459 647 233 36 351 261 90 524 607 136 234 576 568 281 212 301 162 219 552 369 123 67 579 472 114 380 242 154 550 18 217 633 497 577 235 370 34 562 647 159 84 121 5 87 447 658 88 99 98 667 210 157 127 187 20 26 16 418 546 10 544

At this point Auntie Maudie popped into Uncle

David's workshop to see how we were getting on.

'Well, Sherlock Holmes,' she said, looking at me, 'solve that little conundrum if you can and we'll all be rich!'

Johnny sighed and said, 'We shall never get to the bottom of this one. Mr T and his liking for coded messages! He's really gone too far this time. Have you any idea how to solve it?' he asked me.

I had to admit that, as far as I could see, it looked pretty hopeless. At least his earlier coded message had been based on letters of the alphabet, which we eventually unscrambled. These numbers looked impossible to work with. They all appeared to be different; how could any message be found in a jumble like this?

If '1' had equalled A and '2' equalled B, etc, at least there could have been a chance of unscrambling the message. But there are only twenty-six letters in the alphabet, and here many of the numbers went into three figures.

Katie had a good look at the numbers and told us that, in fact, a few of the numbers were repeated. For example, 84 appeared three times.

'I think this message will need a lot more thought,' I told the others. 'I have had enough excitement for one day, let's give it a rest for now.'

'Yes,' Katie agreed, 'I suggest we put it to one side and give it more thought when we are not so tired.'

Sunday 6th March

Got up late after a tiring day yesterday. Had to do some French homework for Mrs Pusscat (her real name is Mrs Catskill, but we call her 'Mrs Pusscat').

Johnny came round after lunch and asked if I had solved our latest code. I told him he must be joking, and anyway I had been busy with schoolwork.

After breakfast, Katie asked if I had had any ideas. 'Are there any similar codes shown in the library book you borrowed?' she asked.

I had to tell her that Johnny and I had just recently taken our library books back, as they had been close to their return date. So we were stuck at the moment, with an undecipherable coded message from the past. Johnny and I agreed to pop to the library tomorrow after school and borrow the same books again.

In the meantime, we took Millie and Chippy out to the park. We gave Chippy some practice at flying around objects such as trees and houses. We had trained him to do this a while ago, when we'd wanted to use him as a sort of drone. We initially needed this to see what a suspected criminal had been doing behind tall hedges. Uncle David made him a mini-camera kit which straps around his chest without hindering his movement. He makes quite a good semi-intelligent drone. I say semi-intelligent as he sometimes goes the wrong way, or sits perched somewhere if he comes across something which catches his interest. Once he came across a parrot in a cage. He disappeared for about five minutes and we began wondering if he had got lost. When we looked back on what he had been filming, we could see he hadn't carried out any spying – he had been too fascinated by the parrot!

Millie found lots of interesting smells when we went through the woods, but no more handbags, thank goodness!

Monday 7th March

As planned, Johnny and I went to the library after school to borrow the books about codes again. Unfortunately, only the one Johnny had borrowed was available. The more comprehensive one was out on loan and was not due back for another two weeks. I put my name down so that it would be put aside for me when it was returned.

When we got home, we looked in the book Johnny had borrowed, but it didn't cover numerical codes, so we seem to be stuck for the moment.

Katie asked us if we had managed to borrow the library books again. I told her we had only found the more basic one and it was no help.

'Well, obviously you need to search on the Internet to see if this type of code is explained there,' she told us.

As Katie had suggested, I looked on the Internet for clues on how to solve number-based codes. I found a site that told us we would need a key text to decipher them.

Johnny reminded me that the message in the jar had also mentioned a third mysterious key.

'So we definitely need some kind of key,' I said. 'And according to this, it will be a bit of text. But what?'

'Oh dear, Mr T and his riddles,' Johnny commented.

As neither of us could think what text was needed, we found Katie and asked her if she had any bright ideas.

'Not at the moment, I don't,' she told us. 'But something might come to me. In a book I've just been reading, a man had a dream, and it gave him the clue he needed to help solve a scientific problem he had been struggling with.'

'So you might dream up an answer for us?' Johnny asked, rather sarcastically. He was obviously not too impressed with Katie's thinking.

When Katie had gone, he said, 'Ben, if your sister hopes to get the answer to our problem in a dream, she must be loopy. We could be waiting until we have long grey beards before she has a breakthrough!'

I agreed that it seemed like grasping at invisible lines in the sky, but you never knew. 'In Biblical times, dreams foretold the coming of plagues of locusts and famine,' I told him.

Tuesday 8th March

Not a lot to write about today. Katie has, so far, not had the magical dream, which she hopes might point to our much-needed key.

Wednesday 9th March

After school, I was working on my maths homework when we had a phone call from Mark Riley, our detective inspector friend. He asked my mum if he could come round tomorrow night and bring a colleague. Also if it would be possible for her to invite Johnny and his parents round. He had an important bit of news for us which at present was all very hush-hush. They would be coming in an unmarked car and could we keep all this to ourselves?

Thursday 10th March

Katie and I were most excited at the prospect of the proposed meeting with Mark Riley and his mysterious colleague. We wondered what the important news was.

At eight o'clock on the dot, Mark and his colleague arrived and, soon after, Johnny and his parents came knocking at the door. Johnny had been kept in the dark about it until he arrived. We had been worried he might mention it at school. ('As if I would!' I can hear him saying!)

Introductions were made. Mark's colleague was introduced as Mr John Brown, although apparently this was not his real name. He was a senior principal at MI5, part of the government's secret service.

Mark said, 'You remember those handbags found in the local woods recently, one of which was found to contain a small gun in a secret compartment?'

'Yes, we remember it well!' Katie, Johnny and I replied in unison.

'My colleague here has had a breakthrough. To cut a long story short, they have traced the owner of the handbag and found that she works for the Slavodamian Embassy in London and is suspected of spying for Slavodamia. However, perhaps a more surprising fact is that we have discovered that she is currently living in a rented house almost directly opposite Johnny and his parents' house.'

'Good gracious!' Johnny's dad said. 'I have seen a lady going in there. In fact, I think there might be two women living there at present.'

'Yes,' Johnny's mum added, 'I've noticed them too. They seem a strange pair. They don't seem to mix with any of our neighbours, they keep themselves very much to themselves.'

'Well,' Mark said, addressing Johnny's parents, 'could you possibly find room to take on a lodger, just for a short time, perhaps a week or two? The person we have in mind is a young lady who like me works for MI5. She is a surveillance officer. Her role when with you would be to keep an eye on your Slavodamian neighbours, to monitor their movements and record who visits their house.'

Johnny's parents looked at each other, and his mum replied that they could manage it at a squeeze. 'We do have a spare room upstairs, which actually faces the street overlooking your mysterious Slavodamian women's house,' she said.

'Well that's excellent,' Mr Brown replied. 'I'm glad you're willing to help us.'

'When does this lady arrive?' Johnny asked.

'As long as your mum and dad are happy with this, she can arrive tomorrow evening.'

'That's okay with me,' Johnny's mum replied. 'I'll have time to clean and tidy the spare room, make up the bed and also find a spare chair or two. Is that okay with you, Reginald?' she asked her husband.

'Yes, perfectly fine with me,' Johnny's dad replied. 'Besides,' he added, 'I will be out at work during weekdays, so won't see as much of her as you.'

Friday 11th March

I met Johnny after school and asked him if his lodger had arrived. He told me that she would be arriving later today. 'After dark,' he added mysteriously. 'It's all very hush-hush of course. Her cover story, if anyone asks, is that she is a distant American cousin of ours, staying for a brief vacation.'

'Can Katie and I come round to meet this secret agent of yours tomorrow?' I asked.

'I expect so,' he replied, 'but I will have to ask her first and let you know.'

Saturday 12th March

Johnny came around this morning and told me that it would be okay to come round about seven o'clock, which would give them time to have their dinner first. He told us that their new lodger had settled in well. As planned, his mum had put her in the front room. She had already set up an office there and got a sophisticated-looking camera on a tripod facing the house opposite. In this way she could monitor every move of the Slavodamians suspected of spying.

'Importantly, she is fluent in the Slavodamian language,' Johnny added.

Katie and I took Millie out for a walk. Chippy came too and had a good time flying around our local park.

At 7.00pm, Katie and I went round to Johnny's house, which is next-door-but-two to ours. Johnny's mum let us in and asked us how we were. She then showed us into the lounge where Johnny was watching TV. His mum got him to switch it off and sent him to find Sonia; this is apparently their new lodger's name. Sonia entered and sat down on the settee opposite Katie and me.

'Hi,' she said, 'I'm Sonia and I believe you two are Katie and Ben.'

Then looking at me, she said, 'I believe you are quite a famous detective, Ben!'

I felt rather embarrassed. I wasn't sure what Johnny had been telling her. He is liable to exaggerate when telling people about our detective exploits.

Then, looking at Katie, she said, 'And I believe you have helped solve quite a few mysteries too.'

Katie replied, saying, 'I'm not sure what Johnny has been saying about us, but you should take it all with a large pinch of salt!'

Sonia smiled and, giving us a quick wink, told us that she was sure it was all true!

Johnny's mum asked us if we would like something to drink. Sonia asked for a Coke, Johnny quickly said he would have the same, whilst Katie and I asked for orange squash.

I asked Sonia how she was getting on with the surveillance work. She replied that she had set up her camera equipment to enable her to get an idea of what the Slavodamians were doing in the house opposite. She was keen to see who their visitors were and establish the pattern of their trips out.

She said she had her camera pointing through a net curtain so that they would not see her watching them.

'What mysteries or crimes have you been investigating lately?' Sonia asked us.

Katie told her how we had been digging for buried treasure in the New Forest.

'Yes, Johnny's mentioned this. He said you had expected to find a buried treasure chest, but only found a jar in a tin!' she replied, grinning.

'Yes, that was rather disappointing,' I admitted. 'But we hope the contents of the jar will lead us to the real thing. You see, we found a coded message in the jar, which could be helpful. The only problem is that it looks extremely complicated and we don't, at present, know how to solve it.'

'That's right,' Katie agreed, 'I fear we may never be able to get to the bottom of this particular mystery.'

I quickly added that we had not given up hope of unravelling the code. And Johnny chimed in, 'We detectives don't easily give up on a case!'

I explained that we had recently managed to break a code with the help of a library book on codes and code breaking.

'Unfortunately,' I said, 'the book we borrowed had to go back to the library and is presently on loan to someone else. We've also searched the Internet to see if we can find out more about the type of code we have. It tells us we need some sort of key, but we have no idea what this key is.'

'It sounds as if your hunt for this treasure is tied

up with someone who likes using coded messages,' Sonia commented.

'That's true,' Johnny replied. 'I found the first coded message in the glove compartment of an old Jaguar in a scrapyard. We're almost certain that it was the car's previous owner who set this code. He was apparently a notorious London gangland criminal.'

'Wow!' Sonia exclaimed, 'you children seem to uncover all sorts of strange goings on! If it's any help, part of my early MI5 training included learning about codes – types of code and how to break them. If you'd like help, I may be able to point you in the right direction with your latest message.'

'Well, that would be great,' I replied.

'If you bring the coded message round tomorrow afternoon, plus any other notes you may have found that were left by this criminal, I'll see what I can do for you.'

When we got home, Mum asked how we had got on with Johnny's new lodger. 'Her name is Sonia,' Katie told her, 'and she seems very nice.'

I added, 'She's going to try and help us solve the coded message we found in the jar from the New Forest. She's a bit of an expert at code breaking.'

'Well that's rather lucky for you,' Mum said.

Sunday 13th March

After lunch, Katie and I visited Johnny's house. We took the latest message we had found in the glass jar, plus the earlier message that we had decoded.

Johnny met us and we went upstairs to the front room where Sonia had set up her office. As she had mentioned, there were net curtains across the windows, so we would not be visible to her neighbours. It was quite a large room. As well as the bed Sonia was using, there was also room for several chairs and a table.

Johnny had the Jaguar owner's manual, so what with my documents and the latest coded message we had found, everything relating to the Trinder codes was to hand.

Sonia looked at the latest code, which was composed entirely of numbers.

'Hmm,' she muttered, 'you've probably noticed that it is made up of many more numbers than the twenty-six letters in the alphabet. Therefore, each letter in the alphabet must be represented by multiple numbers. The most likely type of code is one called the "book cipher". This type of code is based on having a key piece of text and basing letters on this.

'The key text can be anything you like. If you hold on one moment, I will make one up for you to show what I mean.'

She paused to think and then wrote out the following paragraph:

'Dear Katie, Hope you are well. My energy levels have been very restricted over the past fortnight. Now just cannot quite get up enthusiasm to improvise on my xylophone. Sincerely yours, Zina. PS, See you soon.'

'The above text can act as the key to any message I may want to send you. This key text is used to give us a coded alphabet by counting the position of the words in the text and using the first letter of each word. The first word is "Dear" so 1 = D. The second word is "Kate" so 2 = K and so on.'

I have reproduced her breakdown of the coded letters below.

1 = D	2 = K	3 = H	4 = Y	5 = A	6 = W
7 = M	8 = E	9 = L	10 = H	11 = B	12 = V
13 = R	14 = O	15 = T	16 = P	17 = F	18 = N
19 = J	20 = C	21 = Q	22 = G	23 = U	24 = E
25 = T	26 = I	27 = O	28 = M	29 = X	30 = S
31 = Y	32 = Z	33 = P	34 = S	35 = Y	36 = S

The numbers and the letters they are coupled with give us an alphabet coded into numbers, as shown below.

A = 5	B = 11	C = 20	D = 1	E = 8 and 24
F = 17	G = 22	H = 3 and 10	I = 26	J = 19
K = 2	L = 9	M = 7 and 28	N = 18	O = 14 and 27
P = 16 and 33	Q = 21	R = 13	S = 30, 34 and 36	T = 15 and 25
U = 23	V = 12	W = 6	X = 29	Y = 4, 31 and 34
Z = 32				

'My short bit of text allows us to produce coded messages, which can only be read easily if you know what the key text is,' Sonia told us.

'What happens when a letter is represented by more than one number?' Katie asked.

'Well, in such cases, when you are coding a message, you can choose any of the numbers to represent that letter. So if the letter occurs more than once in the message you are coding, you pick different numbers to represent it as you go along. This makes deciphering the message close to impossible unless you have the key text.'

'The longer the key text, the safer the coded message is from being deciphered. Looking at the coded message you found in the buried jar, it looks as if a long key text *has* been used, as the number of words used in this text is 675. This is the highest number I can find. Not that all of those numbers will have been used for coding. In fact, doing a rough count of the numbers in your coded message, only about 150 words have actually been used.

'Now, of course, the problem is knowing what the key text is. If we can discover this, we can begin the task of reading the hidden message. So does anyone know what the key text is?' Sonia asked us.

None of us had any idea what it was. (Katie had not had the magical dream she'd hoped for!)

'Has Mr Trinder dropped any hints in his earlier

message, for example?' Sonia prompted.

We all looked puzzled.

'Well, let's have look at what he has said,' Sonia suggested. 'There may be a cryptic clue or two as to what this key text might be.'

Johnny passed her the Jaguar owner's manual, open at the page showing the earlier coded message. Sonia looked at it and said, 'You did well to solve this, especially as you told me it wasn't a simple substitution code.'

She then looked at Mr T's sketch map and said, 'You must have had some fun with this treasure map.'

We agreed we had, and told her how we had spent a day in the New Forest, travelling in Auntie Maudie's camper van.

Sonia turned the page and read Mr Trinder's rather odd note. '"If this car causes much more offence I will travel to the island of treasure by rail",' she read out.

'I can see his reference to rail fence codes. Your Mr Trinder certainly seems to like talking in riddles, doesn't he? And did you not notice his big clue as to what book he might have been thinking about for his second coded message?'

We were all still rather puzzled. To us, apart from rails and fence, Mr T's words meant very little, least of all what book he was referring to.

'Perhaps it's a generational thing,' Sonia said. 'When I was small, I loved reading a book called *Treasure Island* by the Scottish author Robert Louis Stevenson. Your Mr Trinder is fascinated by the idea of buried treasure and bullion, not to mention drawing treasure maps. In that book, the heroes set off to sea, armed with a treasure map they have found. And they search for buried gold on a deserted island. Mr Trinder's choice of *Treasure Island* as his key text is almost a certainty. It is very appropriate, don't you think?'

We had to agree: it did seem obvious now.

'So we have to get hold of a copy of this book,' Katie commented.

'Yes!' Sonia replied.

'Thanks so much for your help,' I told Sonia. 'If we can do anything to help you, let us know.'

'Well, as a matter of fact there might be something you could help me with,' she replied. 'I have heard all about your remarkable sparrow Chippy, from Johnny. I think he might just be able to help me. First I have to see if I can get hold of a bit of miniature kit from headquarters.'

It all sounded very fascinating.

Monday 14th March

After school, Johnny and I went to the library and managed to borrow a copy of *Treasure Island*.

We then went to Johnny's house, taking Millie and Chippy. Chippy alighted on one or two rooftops on the way, including the Slavodamian women's. We went up to Johnny's bedroom and, opening his window, whistled for Chippy to come. He soon arrived and flew in as he had done many times before. Johnny and I send each other secret messages from time to time using Chippy as a miniature carrier pigeon. He has learnt to tap on windows with his beak, asking to be let in, with a reward of cake crumbs!

We then tapped on Sonia's door.

'Hi, boys, how are you doing?' she asked.

'We've brought you a visitor,' Johnny told her, and as he said so, Chippy arrived and sat on my shoulder.

'Goodness me, what a smart bird you have,' she commented.

'How do you think Chippy could help you?' Johnny asked.

'I've noticed that the Slavodamian ladies over the road are operating mainly from their front room upstairs. I can see them from here using my high-powered lens. Even though it's still only mid-March, we have had some quite warm weather and they frequently leave their window open. Johnny has mentioned that on one occasion you managed to get Chippy to carry a message attached to a small item of jewellery to a location you had pointed to. I wonder if he could carry a small item in through that window of theirs and drop it high up, onto a cupboard at the back of their room?'

'Wow!' Johnny cried. 'Would it have a message attached like, "Look out I am watching you?"'

'No, of course not!' Sonia replied, looking more than a little put out. 'That is the very thing I'm avoiding. I don't want them to know I have them under surveillance.'

'I was only joking,' Johnny quickly added, looking a bit sheepish.

'I am hoping Chippy can fly in their window and drop a small listening device where it won't be seen. This device will then allow me to hear what they are talking about.' Sonia told us.

'Yay!' Johnny exclaimed.

'I think we could manage to get Chippy to do it if we give him plenty of cake!' I replied.

'Oh!' Sonia responded. 'He likes encouraging with little treats, does he?'

'You bet,' Johnny told her.

'However, we shall need to train Chippy to take small items in his beak and drop them onto high cupboards. He's not used to flying through unfamiliar windows.' I told Sonia.

'Not too easy, I guess,' she replied.

'What size and shape will the item be?' I enquired.

'About the size of a hazelnut,' she told me.

'Can it have a small handle for Chippy to grip in his beak?' I asked.

'I will ask our secret gadget workshop to add this,' she said. 'Changing the subject, how is your code breaking going?'

'Well, we've borrowed a copy of *Treasure Island* from the library,' I told her.

'But we haven't had time to work on the code yet,' Johnny added.

'There is a bit of a problem,' I told her. 'Ideally we would like to be able to write numbers next to at least some of the words in the text. This would allow us to count and number them just once, and save having to laboriously keep counting them over and over again. As you noticed, we have numbers as high as 675. Of course we cannot write numbers on the library book pages; also the letter size used in the book is quite small. What we really need is an enlarged photocopy of the first two or three pages so that we can write some numbers next to the words in the text. Even if we only label every tenth word this will save an awful lot of recounting. Besides, we are bound to make a few mistakes when we count. By labelling the letters we can double check we have made no mistakes. Then we can look up each number in the coded message found in the jar, and see what word it is linked to.'

'Well I can help you with that,' Sonia replied. 'I have a scanner-printer attached to my computer and can make enlarged copies for you to work with. If Johnny drops the book over to me tomorrow morning, I can have this ready for you when you return home from school.'

Tuesday 15th March

Johnny collected *Treasure Island* from my house last night, so hopefully we shall have enlarged copies of the first three pages of it by this evening. I counted the number of words on these three pages and it came to well over eight hundred – more than enough for us to crack our number-based code.

Fortunately, I didn't have any homework this evening, as our English teacher was off sick. Johnny came over after he had eaten his dinner and we set to work on the coded message.

He had an enlarged copy of pages one, two and three of *Treasure Island*.

We were a little uncertain whether to include the words "Chapter One" or a subheading of eight words about an old sea dog in our count. We decided to leave these out for now as they were not really part of the main text which followed. We counted the words and wrote ten above the tenth word and twenty above the twentieth, and so on all the way up to the six hundred and eightieth word. It took quite a while to do, plus double checking our counting. We found we had made several mistakes initially but soon put these right. We were now in a position to look up each individual word by number, and using the first letter of each of these words, we were able to write down the decoded message.

Initially we wrote down the first thirty letters

before trying to read what they spelt out.

The message we got was as follows:

'SSOVAIHUDADIFHTHATTIABTFWOPTAC.'

Adding some possible gaps between words it read:

'Ssov a I hu dad I fh that tiab tf wop tac.'

Whilst we could find the odd sensible word like "I" and "dad", overall it just amounted to a lot of nonsense. It was therefore not worth trying to decode any more of the message this way. The key text we were using was obviously incorrect. We looked at the effect of including the chapter subheading in decoding the message, but again it created a nonsense script. The same happened when we included the words "Chapter One".

By this time, we were beginning to wonder if *Treasure Island* was the correct key to use to unravel the coded message.

I picked up the piece of paper we had found in the jar and we both had another look at it. The plain text which came before the coded number message was as follows:

'I have decided that anyone with a metal detector out hunting coins, etcetera, could stumble across my booty by chance. So rather than risk placing it here I have decided it should be hidden in a safer place. So chapter two of this affair will be one of the keys to locating the booty. The others are enclosed.'

'Mr T seems to be dropping hints again,' I said. 'Do you think that his use of the words "chapter two" not only refer to our needing to go on another treasure hunt, but to using chapter two of *Treasure Island*?

Katie had been wondering how we were getting on with our latest deciphering job and had popped in to see how it was going. She agreed that my suggestion was highly likely.

She said, 'I don't think he would have used the word "chapter" otherwise. He would have been more likely to say something like "the second part to this business will be..."'

'So you need me to get an enlarged photocopy of pages one to three of chapter two now?' Johnny queried.

We agreed this was needed.

'Okay, I'll see Sonia and try and get it ready by tomorrow evening,' Johnny told us.

We decided to take Chippy and Millie for a walk. We couldn't go to the park, since by this time it was quite dark, so we went 'round the block', where there is plenty of street lighting. As I may have mentioned before, Chippy is not too keen on going out at night. His instincts make him fearful of being attacked by owls and other night-time predators. He therefore kept close to us and flew from streetlight to streetlight. On the way, Johnny and I discussed how we could train Chippy to fly in through an open window and deposit a bugging microphone on a cupboard.

He has carried small objects in his beak before, but always from one person to another, not to deposit them in a selected spot. He does, however, seem to feel comfortable perching on high shelves. Whether we could get him to fly into the open window of a strange house and put something on a tall cupboard, though, was questionable.

Johnny suggested we try and get him to put a small toy car on my bookshelf, with the prize of a bit of cake up there to entice him. He reckoned if we put a thin piece of wire round the car to make a loop, Chippy could hold this in his beak.

By now it was getting quite late so we decided to leave this problem until another time. We were hoping to examine chapter two of *Treasure Island* tomorrow.

Wednesday 16th March

I had quite a bit of homework tonight. Therefore, when Johnny came over with an enlarged copy of the first few pages of chapter two from *Treasure Island*, I got him to work on them.

First of all, he started by counting the words in this chapter. As with chapter one I got him to label every tenth word he counted.

This was quite a task, what with double checking for mistakes every so often. It took him about an hour to reach the six hundred and eightieth word, which, as before, was as high as was needed. By this time, I had finished my homework.

After this we began using his findings to decipher the coded message. The first number in the message was 277. To find out what letter this represented we looked up the two hundred and seventieth word and then counted seven more. In fact, it was the word 'I'. So 277 was decoded as 'I'. The second number in our coded message was 447. Using Johnny's counting, we found this was the word 'particularly'. So taking its first letter, 447 was decoded as the letter 'P'.

We continued decoding in this manner for another ten minutes and began to see that a clear message was at last emerging. It seemed to be about Mr Trinder buying a cottage somewhere.

At this point we were both quite tired, so I said to Johnny, 'Let's have a break from this decoding.

Did you bring your little toy car with you?'

'Yes, I did,' he replied and took it out of his pocket. He had made a good job of attaching a thin wire loop to its roof.

I called Chippy down from his box on my top shelf and showed it to him. He did not seem too impressed by it at first. He tried pecking at it and decided it was non-edible. However, when I lifted it up by its loop with a pencil and said, 'Look, Chippy,' he decided it might be worth seeing what he could do with it. He picked it up and I told him, 'Take to Johnny.' Johnny called him over so he flew with it to Johnny. He was rewarded with a bit of cake. We went through this procedure a few more times and Chippy became very happy to transport the car from one of us to the other. The more trips he made, the more cake crumbs he got!

Then we got Chippy to take it up to my top shelf by holding a bit of cake above it. At first, he dropped the car and flew to get the cake, but when we didn't give it to him, he realised what was needed for a reward. He is a quick learner and was soon flying with the car, which he would drop on the shelf in order to scoop up a bit of cake.

Saturday 19th March

I've skipped several days writing my diary. Johnny and I have progressed well with Chippy's training. We've got to the stage where he can fly from the road, through an open window into a room, then drop the model car on a cupboard. He is rewarded each time by finding a cake crumb on the cupboard top. This has been tested in both mine and Johnny's houses. He has even done it in Gran's house in a nearby street. To help Chippy know which house he has to visit, I stand at the front door. Then once he has seen where I am standing, Johnny gives him the car and sends him on his way, saying, 'Find cake, Chippy.' He then flies up through the open upstairs window and exchanges the car for the piece of cake, which we have placed on top of a cupboard or shelf.

This morning Johnny came over after breakfast. Katie asked us how we were getting on training Chippy. She asked if we thought it would work if there was no cake on the cupboard for Chippy to find. I told her that hopefully he would still drop the object he was carrying and return to have his cake from me or Johnny.

'And how do you propose to target the Slavodamian women's house?' she asked. 'You told me you had to stand at the house's front door for Chippy to know where to go.'

'Ah!' I replied. 'We've thought of a cunning plan which will take me to their front door!'

Johnny laughed and did a little skip. He loves cunning plans!

'Well I hope it works and you don't get into trouble!' she answered. 'And how are you two getting on with cracking the coded message we found in the jar?'

'We have deciphered the first thirty words. This time the message makes sense. It seems Mr T purchased a cottage somewhere, but we haven't got any further. We hope to have another go at it tonight, but it takes time to go through all the numbers, so we may have to leave it for the time being.'

Katie offered to work on it in order to speed things up, and we gave her the rest of the job to finish. Johnny told her that it would be just as well if she double checked that he had counted all the words correctly before completing the work. It had seemed okay for the bit of text we had decoded so far, but we felt it was as well to be sure we had counted correctly.

We were pleased Katie was going to help us. We just hoped that Mr T had counted accurately in the first place. He had made at least one mistake with his earlier instructions, getting his New Forest map reference a bit muddled.

This afternoon, I went to Johnny's house. Chippy flew with me and tapped on Johnny's bedroom window to be let in.

Sonia told Johnny that the bug was ready for Chippy

to transport. She showed it to us. It looked very much like a small, old-fashioned lady's brooch. It had a clip on the back which Chippy could hold in his beak.

'The hope is,' she said, 'that if the women over the road do find it, they won't throw it out, as it looks quite valuable. They will, with a bit of luck, think it was mistakenly left in the house by a previous occupier.'

We got Chippy to pick it up, which he did, but after deciding it was not edible, he dropped it!

'Not a good start,' Johnny said, but after we had given him some cake, Chippy felt better about it, flew up onto a cupboard and dropped it on top, and was rewarded with some more nourishment.

'So are we set to try and get it delivered over the road?' Sonia asked. 'I see they have left their window open. The device is switched on and I can hear any sound its microphone picks up on my headphones.' She pointed to some on her desk. 'I can also turn my receiver onto speaker mode so that more than one person can hear what is going on.'

She offered the headphones to me and, wearing them, I could clearly hear her as she said, 'Testing one, two, three!'

'It seems that one of the ladies over the road is the main user of their upstairs office,' Sonia told us once I had taken the headphones off again. 'I think she must be in charge, and the other one is there mainly to act as cook and housekeeper.'

'I hope to distract the boss-lady whilst Chippy is visiting so that she won't notice him flying in their office window,' I told her.

'I will leave that to you, Ben,' she told me, 'but be careful. In my opinion, they are a dangerous pair.'

Well, our placement of the bugging brooch went pretty well, but not without experiencing some of what Sonia had warned me about – the Slavodamians are a nasty pair.

There is a new pizza parlour that's just opened locally. I popped in there earlier and asked if they had any advertising leaflets that I could put through people's doors in my area of town. They happily gave me about fifty copies and thanked me for my help, giving me ten pounds for my efforts. They had been planning to get someone to do this, but I had saved them finding someone for my area.

Armed with a bag to put these leaflets in, I began popping them through the doors in our street. When I got to the Slavodamian ladies' house, I became a bit clumsy and, on trying to pop one through their letterbox, knocked on the door and dropped half the leaflets on the ground. Johnny, who was stationed behind a bush in his garden, showed me standing at the front door to Chippy and said, 'Find cake, Chippy,' his signal to fly off and place the object in his beak on top of a cupboard. By my knocking on the door of the house,

I hoped that the Slavodamian ladies would come and answer it, or at least have their attention diverted.

A rather stout, plain-looking woman came to the door and asked, 'Vot you vont?'

I told her I was delivering leaflets. I then heard the other lady calling from upstairs. She shouted something in a foreign language and after a short conversation joined the first lady at the front door.

'What you doing?' she asked me.

'I'm delivering leaflets advertising a new pizza parlour,' I told her.

'Why you knock at our front door?' she asked.

'It was an accident. When some of the leaflets slipped out of my hand, I caught the door knocker whilst trying to catch them,' I told her.

'A likely story,' she said, 'you troublemaker.' She tore up the leaflet I had put through her door, and thrust it back at me.

'We no like small boys and we no like pizzas,' she shouted. 'Go away and no come back.' So saying, she slammed the door in my face.

However, the good news is that Chippy had had a clear run in through the upstairs window, and as far as Sonia could see through her telescopic equipment, the brooch had been dropped just where she had hoped. She had watched as Chippy had hunted unsuccessfully for some cake. Then hearing shouting downstairs, he had wisely made a rapid retreat back to Johnny.

Sonia had heard the disturbance I had caused at the front door. Then she had heard the two women grumbling about nasty children, as they both climbed the stairs to the study. The bugging device was obviously working well. She could now record things like the two women talking and any phone calls they made.

She is very pleased with Chippy's efforts. She is going to nominate him as an assistant MI5 member with a badge to prove it!

Sunday 20th March

Johnny came to see me this afternoon. He told me that Sonia is getting a lot of useful information from the bugging device. She is noting down details of other agents the Slavodamian women get in touch with.

'All this is of course TOP SECRET!' he added. 'So we must not tell anyone.'

For once he was looking very serious.

As usual we went to the park to give Millie and Chippy some exercise. We also went through the woods, where we had found the handbags several weeks ago. Millie likes sniffing everything in there, but remains wary of strangers, following the unfortunate kidnapping episode several months ago.

Monday 21st March

Johnny came round this evening, as I had let him know Katie had finished working on the rest of the coded message, which we had all helped decipher. He was very keen to see what it said.

Katie joined us and told Johnny that it looked as if we were going to have to make a trip to Wales if we were going to find the treasure.

'Cool!' Johnny commented.

'Might be wet as well!' Katie joked, knowing Johnny wasn't really talking about the Welsh weather.

'Anyway, let me read you the message,' Katie said.

'I purchased a cottage at Cwmbwlch near Llanidloes,' she read out. 'I let my dear friend Myfanwy Pugh live there. The gold is in a double padlocked shed, safe code is two four two nine. Tell MP, "Trevor has a new dog."

'I have put punctuation in as best I could,' Katie said. 'It wasn't easy with place names like Cwmbwlch. It contains not one single vowel, so how on earth it's pronounced, I do not know!'

'Are you sure it's correct?' I asked her.

'Well, yes. I found it listed in the index of place names at the back of an old road atlas. With a name like that, it's of course in Wales, mid-Wales to be precise. I found exactly where on one of the atlas's maps.'

'Perhaps this is a trip we could make in the Easter holidays,' I suggested.

Katie agreed, 'Let's ask Auntie Maudie if she is up for a short Welsh holiday in Connie.'

'Yay, cool!' Johnny shouted.

'And possibly wet,' Katie added again, going back to her climatic theme!

I told Johnny, 'I think Katie has a thing about it always raining in Wales.'

Tuesday 22nd March

Auntie Maudie was intrigued by our latest treasure hunt idea. She is all for taking us to mid-Wales in Connie.

'We could do a bit of sightseeing too whilst we're there,' she said.

She is going to look up campsites near Llanidloes, which is the nearest town to Cwmbwlch.

Friday 25th March

This week seems to have gone quickly. Katie and I went to Johnny's house after school. He said Sonia had some important things she wanted to tell us.

Sonia took us up to her office. She said that the bugging device had worked very well and had led to several important findings. Listening to conversations over the road, she had discovered that the two Slavodamian ladies were definitely dangerous spies. They were about to receive vital secret plans from a person working at a government-run design unit. This unit was engaged in drawing up plans for a new nuclear-powered submarine. The Slavodamian Embassy was paying a large sum of money to an employee at the unit in exchange for detailed copies of the plans.

Apparently the spies over the road are expecting a small package containing a memory chip, with copies of the plans on it, tomorrow morning (Saturday). This package will be arriving by special courier. As the two ladies have previously gone shopping on Saturday morning, Sonia told us that she hopes they will be out tomorrow morning. If they are, she will wait until they have left home and, using a skeleton key, let herself into their house. She will then wait for the package to arrive and then substitute the memory chip in it with a blank one of her own.

'Sounds a clever plan,' I told her.

'However,' Sonia said, 'it would be useful if you could act as lookouts. I need to be warned if the ladies return unexpectedly, before I have a chance to switch the chips. I will wear a microphone and receiver so that we can communicate with each other. The idea is for you to watch from my upstairs office. That way, if you spot the ladies returning before I have left their house, you can warn me. I can then quickly escape by their back door.'

She also gave us a contact number for Mr Brown, the MI5 agent Mark Riley introduced us to.

'If any major problems arise and I am not available, please phone him rather than the police. The Slavodamian ladies are foreign diplomats; arresting them without good reason could lead to an international incident,' Sonia told us.

Johnny and I agreed we would be available to help her at half-past eight tomorrow morning.

Sonia thought it would be best if Katie stayed at home but remained ready as backup. If called upon she could then come over with Millie to help.

Saturday 26th March

Today started bright and sunny. By eight thirty I went to Johnny's house, ready to act as a lookout for Sonia.

Sonia ushered me and Johnny into her upstairs office, which had a good view of the Slavodamian ladies' house. As we had already noted, the net curtains in her room keep anyone in there from being seen by the two women. She told us that they had not gone out shopping yet; neither had the expected package been delivered. She had checked her camera footage of their house, filmed that morning, and there had been no activity at all so far.

Just a few minutes later, Sonia said, 'Ah! The ladies are setting off to the shops as I hoped. When they go shopping they normally walk, preferring to leave their car behind.

'Hello! Oh! That's torn it: the delivery man has arrived and handed them the package. What will they do next?'

We could see the delivery van disappearing around the corner, leaving the two ladies in their front garden looking at the small parcel.

'Oh! They've decided to take the package indoors,' Sonia muttered.

The front door shut behind them. 'Bother! They may stay and send the information from the memory chip to their embassy boss in London straight away,'

Sonia groaned.

We could see one of the ladies enter their upstairs office. She went to her desk by the window and placed the package on it. She seemed to hesitate for a moment, perhaps deciding what to do next. Then she turned and left the room. We then saw them setting off again with their shopping bags.

'That's lucky,' Sonia said. 'All I need to do now is slip into their house, open the package and switch the chips over, then make a hasty retreat. I have my earphones and microphone; I can therefore communicate with you if needed and vice versa.'

We saw her cross the road and after a very short pause she unlocked the front door and let herself in. She soon reappeared upstairs.

However, at this critical moment the two Slavodamian ladies reappeared at the corner of the road.

'Watch out!' I called to Sonia on my intercom. 'The ladies are coming back. They must have forgotten something.'

'Okay, get Katie to walk past this house with Millie, pretending to be walking the dog. I may have to throw the package out of the window for it to be rescued. Hopefully Millie can then collect it and Katie can hide it. The ladies may not realise I'm here, find whatever they forgot earlier and go out again.'

It was a tense moment when we saw the ladies

re-enter their house. Very soon Sonia told us she had barricaded the door of the room in case they came upstairs. We then heard a lot of shouting; Sonia had obviously been discovered.

'Vee know you are in there, open zee door,' came the loud voice of one of the spy women.

The window of the room was thrown open, followed by the package being tossed out. It flew through the air into the front garden. The timing was perfect. At that moment Katie appeared with Millie. Millie, who comes from a long line of gundog retrievers, must have seen the package dropping through the air onto the front lawn. She immediately ran in and grabbed it, taking it back to Katie, who quickly set off back the way she had come. She would presumably hide the package somewhere safe at home.

We then heard from our intercom the sound of a door shattering and could see the women enter their office. One of them was waving a gun. She shouted, 'Where is it?' to Sonia.

'Sonia's in trouble,' I called to Johnny. 'I'll ring Mr Brown, Sonia's MI5 boss.'

While I was doing this Johnny told me that the spies over the road must have removed Sonia's microphone as it had gone dead.

He then remembered the bugging device Chippy had planted on their cupboard. He found the headphones for that and its receiver box. He switched it over to loudspeaker mode.

I told Johnny, 'Mr Brown and his men are on their way. They should be here in twenty minutes.'

In the meantime, we could hear the nasty women over the road threatening to shoot Sonia if she did not tell them where the package had gone.

'Try looking in the garden,' she suggested.

They had noticed the window still open and one had gone out to look in the garden but, not seeing the package there, had returned indoors.

This had wasted several minutes, but we were worried Mr Brown would be too late to help Sonia.

I noticed a can of pepper spray on a shelf in Sonia's room, which gave me an idea.

'Come on, Johnny, we've got to distract these old witches.'

I grabbed the pepper spray and we crossed the road to the Slavodamian women's house. You go round the back, Johnny, and when you hear me shout, throw a brick through the back door window. That should unnerve them.'

He went to back of the house to look for a brick and I knocked loudly on the front door.

After knocking several times, as there was no response, I picked up a large stone and banged very hard with it on the front door. This had the desired effect, and a very cross-looking woman holding a pistol answered the door.

'Oh, it's you again, I told you, I no like pizzas!'

'I have a present for you this time,' I replied, holding the pepper spray behind my back.

She lowered the pistol and with one quick action I brought out the pepper spray and fired it straight into her eyes. At the same time, I side-stepped in case she fired at where I had been standing.

She yelled and I shouted to Johnny.

He threw the brick he had found through the back door window. With a great crash the glass shattered. The temporarily blinded woman at the front door swung round in the direction of the glass-shattering noise and fired off one or two wild shots.

I dropped to the floor muttering to myself, 'Random!' as the bullets went all over the place except, fortunately, near me or Johnny. I then quickly crawled past her and up the stairs. They had locked Sonia in a back room. I could hear her shouting to be let out. Luckily the women had left the key in the lock on the outside. I unlocked it and Sonia joined me at the top of the stairs. The blinded woman with her gun had started to climb them, feeling her way as she ascended. I whispered in Sonia's ear, 'Pepper spray.' She grinned and put a finger to her lips, indicating we should keep quiet. She then pulled me back behind her, and waited at the bend at the top of the stairs. The woman reached the top step holding the gun out in front of her. With one swift movement, Sonia grabbed her wrist and, knocking the gun out of her hand, twisted her arm up behind her back. She then marched her past the shattered door into her front room office.

'Get the Sellotape,' she shouted to me.

I grabbed the tape, which was in plain sight on a desk, and we soon had the woman's hands tied firmly behind her back with multiple layers of tape.

Wondering what had happened to Johnny, I looked out of a back window and could see him being chased round the back garden by the second woman. She was waving a broomstick. *Yes*, I thought, *she is definitely a witch, a wicked one at that!*

'I vill kill you, you little vagamuving!' she was shouting. However, it did not look as if Johnny would be caught as he was running much faster than his pursuer.

At this moment, amidst all this activity, Mr Brown arrived with two of his colleagues, followed shortly after by the police in the shape of Mark Riley and several other officers. He had been alerted by one of the neighbours, who had been alarmed on hearing shouting and gunshots.

Both spies were soon put in handcuffs, the tape having been removed from the first one's wrists. She was treated for the temporary effects of the pepper spray. Her eyes remained swollen, but she was now able to see again. They were then led out to a large black van and locked inside by two of the police.

Then Mr Brown, Sonia and Mark went into a back room and closed the door. They obviously wanted to talk privately. When they came out they told us that they had decided that the spies should be deported back to Slavodamia. Their boss, the Slavodamian ambassador, would be firmly warned against any further spying.

Mr Brown's men then searched the house. They removed a considerable number of papers, computers and other equipment. Then all that was left to do was to retrieve the package Katie had hidden at home. Following this they left.

Sonia returned with us over the road to Johnny's

house. Johnny's mum gave us all some lunch. Sonia was very pleased with the help we had given her.

'Ben, you were very brave facing that armed woman. It saved me being tortured or even worse. However, I don't recommend that you ever repeat that kind of thing. It could have turned out very differently.'

After we had eaten, Sonia asked Johnny and I how we were getting on with the code breaking. 'Have those enlarged pages from *Treasure Island* helped you break the code?' she asked.

We told her that they had indeed helped us to crack the code and that we were planning a holiday in Wales.

'This is where the coded message told us we'd find what we're looking for,' I said.

Sonia grinned and said, 'Good luck with your searches, it sounds as if you're on a regular treasure hunt. Perhaps you will come across a third code to break and have to search in yet another location!'

Johnny groaned and said, 'I hope not, I'm beginning to think Mr T is having a laugh at our expense and we're being led up the garden path.'

I agreed it was perhaps the sort of joke he might have enjoyed playing on his criminal mates some forty or more years ago.

'Perhaps he's up there looking down at you now with a wide grin on his face!' Sonia suggested.

Sunday 27th March

Today Sonia left Johnny's house to return back home.

Before she left, she came and said goodbye to me and Katie and thanked us for all our support.

We were sad to see her go. It had been quite thrilling working with the secret service, and helping to catch those two horrid foreign spies.

Things seemed a bit flat after she had gone. Johnny came round and we played a few games on my Progax 4 until it was lunchtime.

This afternoon we took Millie and Chippy to the park and got Millie to play fetch. Chippy as usual tried to help, but was unable to do more than peck at the ball.

Monday 28th March

After school, Auntie Maudie came to see us in Connie, and we discussed our trip to mid-Wales next week, when our Easter holidays begin.

It was agreed we would set off on Saturday morning. Auntie had been doing some research and found a handy campsite near our destination. Uncle David was busy working, so he would not be able to join us this time; Gran, however, was able to come. Johnny already had permission from his mum and dad to come with us too. They were going to have a short break in Manchester, as Johnny's dad had work to do up there for the engineering company he works for.

Friday 1st April

First of April – April Fools' Day today! I was on a careful look out this morning, in case anyone tried playing tricks on me.

One of the girls in our class put some drawing pins on Mrs Standish's chair, as English was our first lesson. She apparently was also on the lookout for pranks. She tipped them off her chair and glared round at the class saying, 'How extraordinary, my chair has pointed to someone being very childish today. I hope whoever is responsible is going to clear up after the lesson is over. We don't want any little pricks trodden on, do we?'

This got a few giggles.

However, Mrs Standish is not one to waste time and promptly got on with our lesson.

This evening, just after we had eaten, we had a surprise visitor. It was Sonia. She came in and Mum made her a cup of tea.

She told us, 'I popped in just to let you know we have caught the person who was trying to pass the secret plans of the new submarine on to the Slavodamian spies. It was one of the secretaries working at the government's design unit. Her fingerprints were found on the chip that Millie and Katie retrieved for me. Also her name was found on some incriminating documents discovered in the spies' study.

'She is at present locked up in Holloway Prison awaiting trial. Her activities will come out in the press when the trial is over, but our names will not be mentioned for obvious security reasons. However, MI5 would like to thank you all for your help, and in gratitude there is a small medal for each of you. There is also one to go on Millie's collar for special occasions.'

Fortunately, Johnny had come round to see about our trip to Wales tomorrow, so he was able to receive his medal too. 'I suggest you keep these medals somewhere safe but out of sight,' Sonia told us. 'Secret agents – even junior ones – should remain anonymous!'

'Does that mean I am a junior sort of James Bond?' Johnny asked.

'Well, yes, in a way, but don't try any of his stunts as seen on cinema screens and TV! In real life spying is rarely so dramatic, even if on occasions risks have to be taken.'

'Yay,' Johnny replied, 'I risked being caught by that nasty woman when she chased me round her garden with a broom!'

'Yes, you were all very brave!' Sonia said with a grin.

Chippy, who had flown downstairs to see what was causing all the chatter, was presented with a very lightweight tag to clip round his neck. He has become an MI5 Wing Commander, for his invaluable and brave placement of a microphone in the Slavodamian spies' office. This had been key to discovering that secret submarine plans were about to be passed to a foreign power.

Saturday 2nd April

We set off on our trip to Wales quite early today and stopped halfway for a picnic lunch at a service station. We got to Llanidloes by mid-afternoon. It is a small town which seems quite a busy place, with lots of shops and pubs, etc. After a bit more shopping, mainly for food, we drove a few miles to our campsite. It overlooks a lovely lake surrounded by hills. We noticed quite a few people out on the water fishing from small white boats. It was all very scenic, so I got out my camera and took some photos.

Fortunately, the weather was dry, which some people consider unusual for Wales. This includes Uncle David and Katie!

It was suggested that to keep things simple we

should have an early fish and chip supper. Gran had noticed a couple of fish and chip shops in Llanidloes. So whilst Johnny and I stayed to put up our tent, the ladies set off to get our supper.

Johnny had decided to have a battered sausage with his chips, Katie wanted scampi and chips whilst the rest of us were having traditional cod and chips.

Our tent was erected and the ground sheet and bedding in place by the time the women-folk returned with our suppers.

'Very good chip shop,' Auntie Maudie commented.

'Freshly cooked fish and the chips, not soggy or undercooked,' Mum agreed.

We ate outdoors. The grownups had brought some directors' chairs to sit on whilst Katie, Johnny and I sat on a rug.

By the time we had finished eating, the sun was setting over the lakeside mountains.

'Red sky at night, shepherd's delight,' Gran quoted, which seemed especially apt as there were lots of sheep on the hills around. Many had newborn lambs with them. The sky was a bright reddish orange, giving a lovely sunset.

We all squeezed into Auntie's camper van to have a cup of tea, or in mine and Johnny's case a glass of pop.

'I hope you have brought all those instructions

about where to find this treasure,' Auntie Maudie said.

'Yes,' I replied. 'I have also got the two keys which were in the glass jar we dug up, along with the coded message. I have also brought with me the library book *Treasure Island*, as I managed to extend the loan period. You never know, we might need it again!'

'Oh no!' Johnny moaned. 'No more codes to decipher, I hope.'

'I hope not too,' I replied, 'but I still have all my notes on decoding the last one we worked on, just in case.'

Sunday 3rd April

After breakfast, we set off to find the unpronounceable village of Cwmbwlch. Fortunately, Connie has an up to date built in sat-nav so we were able to put in the village name. After negotiating quite a few narrow lanes, with twisty bends and few passing places, we managed to find Cwmbwlch.

It was more of a hamlet than a village. There were only a few houses in it, together with several outlying farms and smallholdings.

We met a man walking his dog and asked him if he knew a Mrs Pugh. He told us he was on holiday there, so he could not help us. However, he added that where he was staying, on a farm just up the hill, the lady there was very helpful. 'She should be able to help you,' he said.

As there was no one else in sight, Auntie Maudie decided to look for this farm.

'Just up the hill, he said,' she remarked.

Mum said, 'I've heard that one before, it could be miles away.'

She was right, we got completely lost in a multitude of narrow lanes, and in the end decided to stop and have a brew up. Connie is a great vehicle: she can supply endless cups of tea, which keeps Gran, Mum and Auntie Maudie happy! Us kids had ginger beer, cool from the fridge.

Feeling refreshed, we decided to go back to Cwmbwlch village and try and get some fresh directions.

We were fortunate this time in that we saw a postman. He told us that there were no Pughs living in Cwmbwlch. Our hearts sank. Had we been sent on a wild goose chase by the long-deceased Charlie Trinder?

As he was quite a young postman, Auntie Maudie wondered whether this Myfanwy Pugh could well have died some years ago. After all, Mr T had written his message forty-odd years ago.

The postman had by now disappeared up the road.

'Quick,' Auntie Maudie said, 'Katie, run up the road and ask the postman if he knows of anyone who has lived in the village for a long time. There might be someone who remembers this Myfanwy Pugh, if she ever existed.'

Soon Katie returned, puffing after her speedy run up the road.

'Yes,' she panted, 'the postman said there was a nice old lady, a Mrs Evans who lives at Ty Coch, a red-brick house at the other end of the village. He said she might be able to help.'

'We'd better not all go and visit this elderly lady. We might scare her if we turn up en-masse, especially if she lives on her own,' Mum suggested.

Gran and Auntie Maudie agreed.

It was decided that Katie and I should go. We found the house easily, and an elderly lady opened the front door to us. She invited us in, saying it was nice to have some young visitors, as she didn't get out much these days, her legs not being what they used to be.

'Well how can I help you?' she asked us.

Katie acted as spokesman, being the oldest. She asked if she had known a Myfanwy Pugh, who had lived nearby some years ago.

'Goodness, yes!' the lady replied. 'She was a pillar of the local chapel. Sang in the choir, she did, and played the organ when old Mr Jones the organist was away. Lovely lady, she was. Yes, indeed to goodness, lovely.'

'Well is she still living near here?' I asked.

'No, she passed away twenty years gone, I would guess,' the lady replied.

'Has she any relations still living around?' Katie asked.

'Yes, her daughter still lives in the same cottage her mum had all those years back. They had a smallholding, you know, like a small farm. The daughter still runs it – mainly free-range hens now. Lovely eggs she sells, but why are you interested?' the old lady asked.

I thought I had better answer quickly as I was not

sure it was a good idea to mention the treasure, and it was possible Katie might.

I said, 'I am a friend of the Trinders and I understand Charlie Trinder used to stay at a bed and breakfast that Mrs Pugh ran.'

'Ha!' she replied. 'You are not the first person who has asked about Myfanwy Pugh, and claimed to be a relative or friend of Charlie Trinder.'

'Oh!' I replied, rather taken aback.

'This is a small village and not much happens without me knowing about it. You will no doubt be another person who thinks there is still treasure hidden up at Myfanwy's old place!'

Katie and I were most embarrassed to have been sussed out so easily.

'Well to be perfectly honest—' I started to say.

'Yes, I think honesty is the best way forward,' the lady said, 'and by the way, what are your names?'

'Well my name is Ben, and this is my sister Katie. You may laugh at this,' I said, 'but I'm a detective.'

The lady looked doubtful.

'I know it may seem odd to you,' Katie said, 'but it's perfectly true. Ben, myself and Ben's friend Johnny have helped the police solve quite a number of crimes.'

'It started when I joined our local Neighbourhood Watch group back at home,' I told her. 'Initially, Johnny and I helped to solve two small local crimes.

One involved cats being stolen, and the other was to do with people's garden plants disappearing during the night. I know this may sound very trivial. However, solving these crimes led to us becoming involved with a couple of much more serious offences.'

'I see,' the lady replied. 'So how is your visit to our little village related to criminal activity?'

'As you might be aware, Charlie Trinder was a fairly infamous London criminal,' I said.

'Yes, I did hear it said that he was a bit of a villain, but he was always very good to Myfanwy.'

'Well, as you may know, he was killed in a car crash many years ago. However, he left behind some messages telling us where he had hidden his stolen bullion. In his first coded message he said that his reason for leaving it was so that, in the event of his death, others might find it. However, since this message was written in a secret code, anyone coming across it probably ignored it as nonsense.'

'And where did you come across these messages, all these years after they must have been written?' the lady asked. She was obviously still doubtful as to whether I was telling the truth.

I explained that my aunt had been taking her old car to be scrapped at a local scrapyard, as it would not pass its road test. My mate Johnny and I had gone with her, and to cut a long story short, we had come across the first of two messages in an old Jaguar.

'This Jaguar had once belonged to Charlie Trinder,' I told her.

'Ah yes, I remember Charlie's old Jaguar,' the lady remarked. 'But how did you break these codes, if no one else had done so already?' She asked.

'Well actually, I don't suppose many people had come across them, as Charlie's car had been locked up in his son's garage for a long time after his death. Also, the first message was hidden away on a page right at the back of the car owner's manual, which was shut in the car's glove compartment. Johnny was the one who actually stumbled across it as he was nosing around inside the car. He showed me the handwritten message and we guessed it was a secret code. We thought it would be fun trying to solve it. The scrapyard owner was amused by our wanting the manual and agreed to sell it to us for one pound. He said it would probably only have been thrown away, as the rest of the car was to be taken apart and the parts sold as spares.'

'So, as well as being detectives, you are also code breakers,' the lady commented. She was perhaps being a bit sarcastic about our detective skills, but she seemed amused by my story. 'And I suppose the decoded message told you to come to Cwmbwlch, where the bullion, as you call it, was hidden.'

'Yes, indirectly it did,' Katie replied. 'You see, it

led us to discovering a second message which did tell us to come here.'

'I see, it all sounds very complicated to me,' the lady replied.

'Well, the first message led to a place in the New Forest, where it indicated the bullion was buried,' I told her. 'When we dug there, instead of bullion, we found a small box. On taking this home we found it contained a second coded message. This was the one which told us the bullion was actually hidden here in Cwmbwlch.'

'Sounds as if you have been on a proper treasure hunt,' the lady commented. 'This is really fascinating. I always wondered if Charlie Trinder had really left any of his ill-gotten treasures here.

'In the early days, I saw him once or twice. He drove about in his very posh Jaguar and sometimes took Myfanwy out in it with him. By the way, you can call me Gwen. And incidentally, there is another reason why Mr Trinder may have left instructions for finding his treasure.'

'Really?' Katie replied. 'What would that be?'

'Well, there is old Welsh folklore concerning the perils of hiding treasure. It warns persons hiding treasure to be sure to leave a message for others, indicating where it has been hidden. Failure so to do will inevitably lead to misfortune falling on the person hiding the treasure.'

'Wow,' I said. 'That's a bit scary. Do you think Charlie Trinder knew of this?'

'I would be surprised if he didn't,' Gwen replied. 'After all, Myfanwy knew he was hiding his valuables at her place, and she would almost certainly have told him.'

'Yes, but if he had told her where it was,' Katie objected, 'he was surely in the clear.'

'That's as may be, my dear, but as I and others in the village knew, she was unable to get at whatever it was, locked up in a safe in a very strong shed. She lacked a key to get into the shed, and in any case, did not know the code number needed to open the safe.

'Anyway,' Gwen said, 'getting back to the present, what has been puzzling me is how did you two get here?'

We told her how our Auntie Maudie had brought us in her camper van. Our mum, gran and Johnny had also come, as we planned to combine the treasure hunt with a holiday in Wales.

'So where are all these other people?' Gwen asked.

'They are parked up just outside,' I replied.

'Oh dear, they will be wondering where you have got to,' Gwen remarked.

We agreed.

'But, before we go out and find them, tell me what you intend to do if you do find this bullion,' she said.

'Well, first of all we shall need to have a word with the police and find out what the normal procedure is for finds of this kind. Is it treasure trove or what?' I said.

'I see,' Gwen replied. 'I think that sounds the best way forward. However, as I said earlier, there has been at least one other person asking how to find Myfanwy. Whatever Charlie Trinder left may already have been taken.'

We accompanied Gwen to her front gate and found Connie parked behind a tall hedge just outside.

Katie introduced Gwen to Auntie Maudie, Gran, Mum and Johnny.

Having made all the introductions, Gwen agreed to show us the way to Myfanwy's old cottage. I think she was intrigued with our tale and wanted to see if any of Trinder's bullion was still there.

It was just as well we were shown the way, as it was up a twisty lane and then along a rather rutted farm track. Myfanwy's daughter was called Bronwyn. She was pleased to see Gwen and greeted her with a hug.

Gwen explained the background to our visit, telling Bronwyn that we youngsters were junior detectives! Bronwyn grinned broadly on hearing this and invited us into her cottage. We were offered tea, which Mum, Gran and Auntie gladly accepted.

Then, looking at me, Bronwyn said, 'Well, young detective, before we go any further, anyone coming here wanting to investigate the so-called bullion must give a secret password or sentence. My mum told me about it just before she went into an old people's home.'

I wracked my brain. What could she be talking about?

Johnny came to the rescue, crying, 'Trevor has a new dog!'

'Ah!' Bronwyn replied. 'Your friend there has got it right! I can tell that you have the correct connections with Charlie Trinder to be allowed to look in his safe.

'After Charlie died we did wonder if anyone would come looking for his safe and his bullion. Well, not long after the news of his death was announced, we had a couple of truly nasty villains visit us. They did not know the password and tied me and Mum up to get to Charlie's safe. It was still there, where he had put it, in a shed out the back. They picked the two big padlocks on the shed door and managed to open the safe.

'However, they weren't best pleased when all they found in it was a packet containing about two hundred pounds in used bank notes and a few meaningless papers. They then came back to us and demanded to know where all the stolen gold bars had gone. We told them we knew nothing and Mum warned them that we were expecting a couple of our friends to drop round any time now. I think this worried them, as my mum had hoped it would! They might have got caught with what cash they had already taken, so they hurriedly left. They were real brutes though; they left us still tied up! Fortunately, a neighbour who regularly came to buy our eggs arrived and untied us. We then went out to the shed and found the door unlocked and the safe door wide open, with just Trinder's old papers left in it. We closed the safe and the shed door, clicking the padlocks shut. It has never been opened since. We always wondered if anyone would turn up with Charlie's password to look in it.

'So you see, there is nothing much left in the safe except a few of Charlie's old papers,' Bronwyn told us.

By now it was past lunchtime, so it we decided to pop down to a pub in the next village for some sandwiches and return later. Gwen came with us; she was also hungry and pleased to be invited to join us. It was a welcome change from her normally quiet way of life, she told us, and she was thrilled to see some exciting action.

After we had eaten, with Gwen's help we found

our way back to Bronwyn's smallholding. She was outside, busy feeding her hens. She greeted us with a wave and told us we could help by collecting the eggs. We were given some small baskets and told where to look for them.

When this was done, she took us indoors and told us that she had a key to one of the padlocks on the shed, adding that we should have the other. One of our two keys did fit, so between us we were able to open the shed door. It was a strong windowless, metal shed, not one which could be got into without the keys or possibly an acetylene cutter.

On a sturdy shelf sat the safe. It was covered with dust and lots of cobwebs. Bronwyn had anticipated this and cleaned it up with a large duster. Our second key opened a lock in the safe door, and then we had to rotate a central knob following the numbers given in Mr Trinder's second coded message: 2 4 2 9. I could hear some plonking sounds within the safe door as I did this. Auntie Maudie told us this was the tumblers in the lock falling into place to allow the door to open.

'I expect those villains who opened it last were expert safe crackers,' she said. 'They usually use a doctor's stethoscope pressed to the door and listen to hear the tumblers drop.'

I wondered how Auntie Maudie knew all this, but then remembered she likes reading whodunit books.

The safe door swung open, and as Bronwyn had warned us, we found it was practically empty, apart from a few old papers.

'This is how we found it all those years ago, after we were released from the villains' ropes,' Bronwyn told us. 'The shock nearly killed my mother; in fact, I think it shortened her life. She suffered ill health ever after and died only three years later. I am so glad you have come. It ends a chapter of uncertainty in my life.'

Johnny, Katie and I were disappointed that the safe contained so little. Although Bronwyn had warned us, we had secretly hoped it might contain a few old coins or other valuables missed by the earlier intruders.

'You can bring those papers into the house and have a look at them whilst I make your mum, auntie and granny another cup of tea and indulge you all in some of my freshly baked cake,' Bronwyn told us.

Chippy, who had been sitting on a branch nearby, perked up at the word cake and flew down to me. Bronwyn was quite amused.

'Does your dog also want a snack or two?' she asked.

Katie told her how Millie normally only had two mealtimes a day.

'But,' Bronwyn pleaded, 'she has been so well

behaved. Even my hens took a liking to her! They normally expect dogs to try and chase them. I think she deserves a little something as a treat. Besides, she's on holiday! She could have one of my dog Tizer's biscuits.'

Tizer was a small Jack Russell terrier. So Tizer and Millie each had a couple of biscuits whilst we had drinks, and Chippy joined us, having a few cake nibbles.

After this we spread the papers from the safe out on a table. Johnny immediately said, 'Oh no! I knew it, there is another coded message!'

Sure enough there was a page with another set of numbers on it. It looked similar to the last coded message, which we had cracked with Sonia's help.

'Perhaps you will have to go off on a further treasure hunt!' Gwen suggested, grinning broadly.

It rather looked as if she might be right.

'I think we have done enough for one day,' Mum suggested. 'We should leave Bronwyn in peace and drop Gwen home. Then we should head back to our campsite.'

Bronwyn said she was delighted we had called and that if we needed further assistance she would try and help. Then she told us we would be welcome to park Connie in a small field behind her house if we wanted to.

'It could save paying fees at a campsite,' she

added.

Auntie Maudie thanked her and said we would have to go back to the campsite tonight, as we had already booked a space for Connie and left a tent there. She would also need to settle the bill for our stay there. However, if it was okay, we would love to come and stay in her field for one or two nights before moving on.

'I will see you all tomorrow then,' Bronwyn called as we set off.

Back at the campsite Mum and Auntie prepared us some tasty omelettes using Connie's cooking facilities. A dozen eggs, which Bronwyn had insisted we take with us, made up the main ingredients.

After we had eaten, Johnny, Katie and I had a look at the coded message we had found in the safe. It was as follows.

555 567 245 351 552 197 130 529 607 16 658 65 99 375 651 219 579 567 232 72 114 576 233 647 146 76 100 59

'Well at least it is shorter than the last one we had,' was Johnny's comment.

'I hope it doesn't tell us to set off on another trip miles from home, like up to Scotland for example,' Katie said. 'Why not try using the *Treasure Island* Chapter Two key again? Mr T may have reused it to save time.'

I dug it out from a folder I had brought with me. It quickly emerged that Katie was spot on. Words emerged that appeared to make sense.

'Wow, well done, Katie!' Johnny shouted. 'This message did use the same key as before.'

After a few minutes of decoding we were able to read the complete brief message. It was a little peculiar. It read as follows: 'Finder take the safe it is special'.

Auntie Maudie was interested to see what it said. '"Finder",' she said. 'That means you kids. You were the finders, especially Johnny who found the original message in the Jaguar manual. "Take the safe it is special." It appears to be telling you to take the safe with you. That seems a bit ridiculous, as it must weigh a ton and would be difficult to transport. I certainly could not put it in Connie. Why would we want it?'

'Because it's special,' Johnny chipped in.

'Did you see anything about it that makes it special?' Auntie Maudie asked.

'No,' we kids agreed, but then, what did we know about safes? It wasn't as if we came across them every day. In fact, I had never seen one close-to before.

'Maybe it contains some gold coins in a hidden secret compartment, like in a false bottom,' Johnny suggested hopefully.

'Well there must be something about it that is out of the ordinary,' I agreed.

We left it like that, and after watching a bit of TV, Johnny and I decided to go to our tent for a well-deserved night's sleep.

'Do you remember our night spent in that haunted vicarage?' I asked Johnny.

'Yes, don't remind me, I might have nightmares,' he replied.

'I'm going to get Millie to join us out here,' I told him. 'She will act as guard and keep us safe from any ghostly Welsh dragons or ghoulish goblins.'

Millie joined us, but Chippy preferred to keep in the warmth of the camper van with Katie, Mum, Auntie and Gran.

Monday 4th April

Millie and Chippy woke us! Chippy had obviously been let out of the camper van and come to find us. Millie, hearing his pecking at the tent flap, had raised the alarm.

I found Chippy a bit of stale cake from my jacket pocket and got dressed quickly. Johnny turned over and decided to have a bit more sleep, but Millie decided otherwise and jumped on him. He muttered, 'Ow, geroff! I was just dreaming that a herd of hairy wild bison were charging at me. You nearly frightened the life out of me, you scary great heffalump!'

I laughed and Johnny decided he had better get dressed. We went to the camper van for breakfast, and then Johnny and I took down our tent. Finally, we set off back to Cwmbwlch to see Bronwyn and find out where we could camp there.

By the way, we've discovered how to pronounce Cwmbwlch. The letter 'w' is a vowel in Welsh and is pronounced roughly as an 'oo'. So it sounds something like Coomboolch. (Note, I say roughly, as I am sure that's not quite right.)

At Cwmbwlch, Bronwyn showed us a field behind her cottage and pointed to a spot where we could park Connie and put up our tent. She then invited us all in for drinks: a cup of tea for the adults and fresh milk for us kids. Bronwyn apparently has her own cow, which she milks by hand early every morning and again in the evening.

'If you get up at six o'clock one morning whilst you are here, you can help me milk Ermintrude. That's my cow's name,' she told us. 'I named her after the cow in the old children's TV programme *The Magic Roundabout*. I loved watching that when I was a youngster. I especially liked Ermintrude the cow. I thought her name was dead cool, as you youngsters would say!'

Katie and I agreed we would help milk Ermintrude. Johnny said he would leave it to us as he was not good first thing in the morning.

Bronwyn then asked us how we had got on with decoding the message we had found in the safe. Had it indicated yet another treasure hunt somewhere else?

I explained that we had indeed managed to decode what it said. And no, there were no instructions for another treasure hunt. However, it had advised us to take the safe with us when we left, as it was rather special and could prove useful!

'Golly,' she said, 'it will take some shifting. It must be pretty heavy.'

Auntie Maudie agreed and repeated what she had said before: it could not go in Connie, as she was loaded up enough with all of us as it was.

Bronwyn told us she would be glad if we did take

it away, as this would close a rather unpleasant chapter in her life. Not to mention she was looking for a new place in which to keep her garden tools. 'The shed would be ideal for that,' she said.

'Tell you what,' she continued, 'I have an uncle who works for a large furniture shop in Llanidloes. They deliver furniture all over the UK. I think for a small fee he could arrange for the safe to be delivered to your home.'

We agreed this would be a great idea – except Mum wondered where we could keep it at our house. Johnny said they had a large shed at the side of his house and thought it could go in there until we had decided what to do with it.

So it was agreed that Bronwyn would ask her uncle to fix up a delivery.

The rest of the day was spent doing a bit of shopping in Llanni (this is the local shorthand name for Llanidloes). Whilst there we bought some sandwiches, crisps and pop for our lunch. We then drove to the nearby Llyn Clywedog reservoir to eat our picnic. I understand the reservoir is named after the river which flows through it, the Afon Clywedog. Johnny likes Welsh places which end in 'dog' – there are quite a few! He thought it appropriate that Millie should go in for a swim!

She needed very little encouragement and leapt in, making quite a splash. Chippy followed closely, observing her progress from above, making sure he didn't get wet like Millie!

Luckily Mum had brought an old towel with which to dry Millie if she got wet. We gave Johnny the job of drying her when she came out. He went to the water's edge as she clambered out and got wet himself as she shook herself, sending water off in all directions, including over him. We had to laugh! He was quite indignant. However, he had been the one encouraging her to go for a swim in the first place.

When we got back to Cwmbwlch, Bronwyn told us that the removal of the safe to Johnny's house had been arranged. The furniture shop delivery men would take the safe there and put it in his shed next time they had a furniture delivery in the area.

Johnny rather belatedly decided he had better phone his mum to check it was okay for the safe to be put in their shed for a short while. Fortunately, according to Johnny, she said it would be 'well... okay.'

Tuesday 5th April

Today we had a trip to find the source of the River Severn. Auntie Maudie parked Connie on the edge of a forest. It's called Hafren Forest. There was a public car park and even a block of toilets. We had made quite an early start, so Gran and Auntie Maudie cooked us some breakfast. Whilst they were doing this, Mum, Katie, Johnny and I went and had a quick look round the immediate area. We found some signposts, one of which pointed to a footpath which said, 'To the Source of the Severn'. It also told us it was a four-hour walk – we assumed this meant it was two hours there and two hours back. We met a couple of people who looked like experienced walkers and they confirmed this was so. They assured us that the long walk was well worthwhile.

We returned to Connie, and over breakfast reported the nature of the walk we had planned. It was decided to put a few sandwiches together and bottles of spring water. We packed these in our rucksacks and set off in search of the place where we expected to see the great River Severn gushing out of the ground high up in the mountains.

Luckily it was a dry day with some hazy cloud high overhead – just right for a long hike.

Millie was excited, as she seemed to realise we were in for a good long walk. Chippy was not so sure. He had spotted one or two large birds circling above and was a little concerned they might attack him. He has had a narrow escape from a large seagull in the past and considers most large birds, apart from pigeons and chickens, a threat. He kept close to us as we walked.

The route took us alongside a wide stream, which we noted from a map was a youthful section of the River Severn. Initially the path was fairly flat and ran along a nice wooden walkway. Then it began to rise uphill fairly steeply in places. For a while it took us up through wooded forestry, then later it emerged from the trees and ran through open rough grassland. All the time our path ran close to the stream, which got narrower as we went along.

Gran, who is not used to walking uphill for long periods, asked us to take a break. We had been walking for over an hour by now. Chippy had also become rather weary, and had been sitting on top of my rucksack chirping away for the past quarter of an hour. We drank some water and after about ten minutes set off again.

The path eventually became less steep and the countryside opened out into moorland high up in the hills. About ten minutes later we saw what we were looking for. There was a wooden post sticking out of the ground with the words 'Source of the Severn' written on it. Rather than finding a river gushing rapidly out of the hillside, we found the source of the Severn consisted of water trickling sluggishly out of the ground in a rather boggy area. Millie decided to have a drink as she was obviously thirsty after her long walk.

I took a photo of the signpost to prove we had got there. Chippy, wanting to show he had been there too, perched himself on top of it!

The views around were great. We could see for miles and Auntie Maudie reckoned one of the mountains we could see was Plynlimon, the highest mountain in mid-Wales.

We agreed it was time to have our lunch, so we found a place to put down a couple of rugs Auntie Maudie had brought and sat down and had our sandwiches.

We didn't see any other walkers. The only other living creatures we saw were sheep; there were quite a few up there, grazing peacefully in amongst the heather. And there were one or two large birds flying high above us.

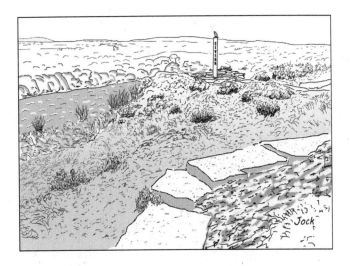

After a short rest we set off back to Connie. The return journey was downhill all the way, so it was much less tiring than it had been coming up. This pleased us all, especially Gran.

Back at Connie we all sat down for a well-deserved rest with cups of tea for the grownups and fruit juice for us kids.

Auntie Maudie asked if we fancied spending the rest of the week exploring a bit more of the Welsh countryside. We had, after all, found what we had come to Wales to find – that is, Mr T's double padlocked shed and safe. We had also arranged for the safe to be transported back to Johnny's house.

'I would like to visit the seaside,' Katie told her. Johnny and I agreed this was a good idea.

So it was decided that we would thank Bronwyn for her hospitality and travel to the Welsh coast. Then depending how we felt, we could visit some other areas of interest before going home. Katie and I said that, before leaving, we would like to help Bronwyn milk Ermintrude, her cow.

Wednesday 6th April

This morning Katie and I got up early to help Bronwyn milk Ermintrude. We had never seen exactly where milk came from! Johnny, who stayed in bed, told us that of course he knew where it came from – from plastic bottles in the supermarket! (He was only joking, I hope...)

Katie and I found it quite slow-going getting milk from Ermintrude, especially at first, but Bronwyn told us we had done well for beginners.

'Some people take ages and cannot get the hang of it at all,' Bronwyn told us. 'On large dairy farms they use milking machines, which makes light work of the job. They can collect milk from several cows at the same time with their machines. You *can* get a machine for milking a single cow, like mine. However, I don't feel I should spend my precious money on one, even though it would make the job quicker and easier.'

By the time we had finished, Katie and I were quite hungry and Bronwyn invited us all into her kitchen for a cooked breakfast of bacon, sausages, fried eggs and fried homemade bread. It was FAB, as Katie remarked. Even the still bleary-eyed Johnny enjoyed it.

Auntie Maudie thanked Bronwyn for everything and told her that, now we had found and opened the safe, we planned to move on and visit a bit more of Wales before returning home. However, we would always be grateful for her help and hospitality. We would of course keep her informed of any developments as to the whereabouts of Mr T's treasure, if it still existed.

So with much waving goodbye and Bronwyn telling us to come again soon, we set off. One of the closest places on the coast, as shown by our map, appeared to be the town of Aberystwyth. So that was where we headed. It turned out to be a bit of a twisty road to get there, with several hold ups on the way. Not by highwaymen, but by road works. However, we arrived at the town in good time for lunch. We found our way round to the seafront and decided that, before going to the beach, we would have a good solid lunch to set us up for the rest of the day. We found a local café and had a sit down meal. There was a good choice of food on their menu. Johnny and I had pizzas, with multiple fillings; Katie had ham, egg and chips and the adults had various pies and chips plus mushy peas (which Katie hates).

After this we went to the beach. It was not very busy and I took a photo of it with Katie and Millie posing in the foreground. The tide was quite well out. We all had a good walk across the sand and some of us, including Millie, went for a paddle in the sea. We decided the water was too cold for a swim, so ran around and kicked a football about.

Millie palled up with a couple of dachshunds she met. Their owners had apparently come from Liverpool for a holiday, as Wales is not too far for them.

We noticed a steep rocky hill rising up from the seafront to the north. It appeared to have a railway running up it. The dachshund's owners told us that it was called Constitution Hill, so named as the walk up it is supposed to be good for your constitution. In other words, it kept you fit!

'Probably fit to drop!' Mum commented, and Gran agreed.

The cliff railway was, we were told, over a hundred years old and was described as a funicular railway. It had two railway carriages on it, attached to each other by a single cable. This ran round a big pulley wheel at the top of the hill. So as one carriage was hauled uphill, the other descended on the other end of the cable.

We decided to go on this railway and made our way to the ticket office at the bottom. Chippy started the journey on my shoulder, but halfway up he flew out of the window and flew next to the train for the rest of the journey.

'Good for his constitution!' Katie commented.

When we got to the top, a railwayman asked if we had enjoyed the ride. He said the carriages were now driven by an electric motor, but when the railway was built it had been run using water. Both carriages had a large water tank. A steam engine pumped water up the hill into the tank in the carriage at the top. The water was then let out from the tank in the bottom carriage and the weight of the water in the top carriage propelled it downwards, hauling the other, now lighter, carriage up. The train had a braking system so that neither carriage could run away in an uncontrolled manner.

There was a café at the top, so of course the grownups went in for cups of tea! Meanwhile Katie, Johnny and I had a wander around outside. As the weather was mild, the view from the top was very good. We could see the town of Aberystwyth below us, and beyond for many miles further south, with views along the Welsh coastline.

Later, having made our way back to Connie, it was agreed to travel north and find a campsite for the night.

Thursday 7th April

Weather still good, and having spent an uneventful night near a place called Dolgellau, we looked at our map. Katie spotted Harlech Castle a little further north. She told me and Johnny that we should have heard of it because there is a well-known song called 'Men of Harlech'. Johnny and I had never heard of the song *or* the castle! However, along with the grownups we agreed that it would be an interesting place to visit. Johnny and I both like exploring old castles. Auntie Maudie said she had been there once before, and it was one of Wales's nicest-looking castles.

'Not particularly large,' she told us, 'but nicely proportioned, like me!' We all had to laugh, as she is rather large.

We arrived at the castle by late morning and noticed there was a modern-looking café opposite, so of course cups of tea and cold drinks were the first requirement. We piled into the café and decided that, although it was a bit early for lunch, we would have some. The café staff apparently sold a range of delicious homemade foods, which was the deciding factor.

We then went to the castle. It has a huge gatehouse, which would have been a formidable barrier to any enemies wanting to gain entrance back in the past. We met a visitor-guide and he told us a bit about the castle's history. As many children know, England was conquered in 1066 by William the Conqueror of France at the battle of Hastings. Harlech Castle was built by one of his successors, King Edward I. It took his workmen just seven years to build. It was completed in the year 1289. The aim was to conquer the unruly Welsh! To help with this plan, three other castles were also built in this general area at the same time. Unsurprisingly, the conquering ruling family, having come from France, used a Frenchman to oversee its planning and building work. The man employed was James of St George; he built it using the local rock. It had a wide moat on two sides, a steep cliff to the north, and to the west it had the sea, which at that time came right up to the castle. So it was pretty impregnable. Today the sea is nearly two miles away, as its level has dropped a fair bit since 1289. Either that or land level has risen – I don't know which. (I must ask Uncle David when we get home.)

Johnny asked if the Welsh had ever managed to capture the castle.

'Yes,' the guide told us. 'In 1404 one of Wales's rebel armies, led by Owain Glyndwr, laid siege to the castle and managed to starve out the English and capture it. They apparently even held a parliament in the castle during the time they had it. However, four years later the English reclaimed it using siege tactics against the Welsh. After that, the castle was used as a fortress by both English sides in the Wars of the Roses.'

Having been given this brief history, Johnny and I could not wait to go exploring.

There were many different sets of stairs running up to the higher battlements. Once up on these we could walk round and take in the views. We could see out to sea and also across to the Snowdonia mountains of north Wales. Katie and Auntie Maudie followed us up to get the views, but Mum decided to stay with Gran and admire the architecture in the lower areas of the castle.

It was late afternoon by the time we set off in Connie again. We decided it was time we returned home. Auntie Maudie phoned Bronwyn at Cwmbwlch and asked if we could stay another night on her farm. This apparently was conveniently on our route home. She said she would be delighted to see us again, so we headed back there.

On our arrival, Bronwyn was pleased to see us all again and her dog Tizer was happy to see Millie. Chippy visited his distant relatives, the chickens, and chirped at them. They, however, largely ignored him and continued looking for worms in Bronwyn's lawn.

Friday 8th April

This morning, Bronwyn invited us into her farmhouse kitchen for a cooked breakfast, which was similar, but even larger, than the last one she had given us.

Mum said that we must pay her for it as this was the second time she had made us breakfast. However, Bronwyn told us she would not hear of being paid.

'What you can do, if you find the missing treasure, is buy me a small milking machine for milking Ermintrude!'

We agreed to do this.

'By the way, Johnny,' Bronwyn said, 'my uncle is going to pick the safe up later today and take it down to your place tomorrow. You should be home by then and can show him exactly whereabouts to put it.'

'That sounds exciting,' I said.

Johnny and Katie agreed. We couldn't wait to have another close look at the safe and see what might be special about it.

Soon after breakfast we set off for home. Auntie Maudie was keen to get underway, as we had a long journey ahead of us. So we said our goodbyes and left.

Saturday 9th April

It was nice to get home again last night and have my own bed to sleep in. Sleeping in the tent was fun at first, but by Thursday I was finding it a bit like trying to sleep on a wooden plank. And I found my feet were cold each morning.

After breakfast I phoned Johnny to see if there was any news of when the safe would be delivered. He said his mum had received a text message saying that the delivery would be around three o'clock this afternoon. So I agreed to go round to his house after lunch so we could play games on his K-box 10 until the delivery men came with the safe.

Just after three, we heard vehicle brakes making a hissing sound, and on looking out saw a large green van had drawn up outside Johnny's house. We hurried downstairs and out into his front garden. Two men jumped out of the van and said, 'Hi, is this the right address for Mrs Addison?'

This being Johnny's mum, we told them it was.

'Well, we have a safe delivery for you,' they told us, grinning.

By this time Johnny's mum and dad had appeared on the scene.

'Where do you want us to put this item?' the men asked. We took them round the side of the house and showed them the bench in the shed.

Wiping the back of his hand across his brow, the man who seemed in charge said, 'Oh dear, no, oh no, that will never do. We will never be able to lift it up onto that bench, it's far too heavy. Besides, the bench might collapse under its weight. I don't know what you've got in it, but it weighs a ton.

'Well, what do you suggest?' Johnny's dad asked.

'Well, if I might make a suggestion the delivery man said, I would move the bench out of the way and we can wheel the safe into your shed and place it on the floor in the corner there. Would that be okay?'

I looked at Johnny and nodded and he told them it would be okay as far as we were concerned, and Johnny's dad agreed he would be happy with it on the floor. I then asked the men if they could leave a gap round the back of it, as we would like to examine it. The men looked at me as if I had gone a bit potty, but Johnny's dad said it was okay as far as he was concerned.

The bench was moved out of the way, and we followed the men back to their lorry to see how they would manage to get this weighty thing out.

They got into the back of the lorry and manoeuvred the safe onto a sturdy sack trolly. This was then wheeled onto a tail-gate lift at the rear of the lorry. The tail-gate was then slowly lowered to the ground. From there they managed to wheel the safe out onto the road and then along a garden path and into the shed. It was then fairly easy to slide the safe off the trolly and onto the shed floor.

'There we are,' the boss-man said, smiling broadly, 'all *safe* and sound.'

Johnny liked this jokey statement and replied, 'A safe safe, safely in a shed, just the job!'

The men apologised that the safe had suffered a slight bit of damage in transit.

'Sorry, folks,' the boss-man said, 'we managed to scuff a bit of paint off one of its corners.' He pointed to the top right-hand corner, where some of the safe's coating of black paint had come off.

'Don't worry,' Johnny's dad replied, 'I expect we can easily find a bit of paint and touch it up.'

Johnny's mum then offered the men cups of tea. They thanked her, but said that this was their last drop off point today and they wanted to get back to Wales before the worst of the rush-hour traffic.

Just after the men had left, Katie and Uncle David arrived. Katie had known the safe was being delivered at about three o'clock and thought Uncle David would like to see it. He had, after all, helped us track it down. She had phoned him, telling him of the expected delivery. She had also mentioned that it was, in some way, special. Intrigued by this, he had joined her and come to see it.

We all went round to the shed. Johnny's dad wanted to see inside it, wondering if we might have missed anything left inside. So as Johnny had the key and knew the combination number, he opened the door.

Considering how heavy the delivery men had found it, Johnny's dad was surprised to see that it was completely empty. I told him that it had just had a few of Charlie Trinder's old papers in it when we'd first found it, and I had taken these home. I added that, apart from the coded message, which we had read, the others did not seem important.

Johnny told his dad that the coded message had simply told the 'finder' to take the safe as it was 'special'.

Wondering what was special about it, Johnny's dad suggested he should tap it all over with something hard to see if it had any hollow-sounding areas.

'There might be secret compartments to hide valuables in,' he suggested.

Uncle David gave him his pen knife and told Johnny to use one end of it to tap the safe.

So Johnny looked inside and tapped all over the sides, top and bottom, with the end of Uncle David's Swiss army knife, but it all seemed solid enough. Then he looked round the back of it and tapped that. This also appeared to be completely solid. In fact, he found no trace of any hollow-sounding areas in which valuable items might be hidden. We were thinking of items such as diamonds or other jewellery. Johnny and I were very disappointed. None of us could see anything special about the safe. It was quite a puzzle and most unsatisfactory considering the coded message left by Charlie Trinder. We had had high hopes that this special safe would turn out to contain the treasure we sought.

'Well, where do we go from here?' Katie asked.

'We could sell it,' Johnny's dad suggested.

'Yes, but we'd need to touch up that scuff mark on the top corner first,' his wife told him.

I hadn't taken much notice of this up to now, but looking at it closely I was surprised to see that, where the paint was missing, the metal below was yellow in colour.

'The safe seems to be made of a yellow metal under the black paint,' I commented. 'Could it be made of brass?'

Katie also had a look and said, 'Hey, it might be

gold!'

'Wowee!' Johnny shouted. 'That's it, it's made of gold – the stolen gold has been melted down and made into a safe!'

His dad said, 'You could be right. Gold is about two and a half times heavier than steel, from which safes are usually made. This would explain its great weight.'

Uncle David agreed.

'I'll go and get a strong magnet,' Johnny's dad said. 'That will show us if it is made of steel or not.'

He soon reappeared with a magnet and found that the safe door was made of steel, but the rest of it was not.

'Perhaps the door with its original locking system came from another safe, but the cunning criminals who had stolen the gold must have had it melted down and cast in the shape of the rest of the safe. When painted it would be a crafty way of hiding the gold in plain sight!' Johnny's dad said.

'Yes, considering whose safe this was, gold does seem to be its likely composition,' Uncle David agreed.

'I think it's time for us to bring in the police,' Johnny's mum suggested.

We all agreed and Katie said, 'Let them test the metal to see what it is and if it *is* gold, they can perhaps suggest who, if anyone, it belongs to now.'

After Katie and I had eaten our dinner we returned to Johnny's house. It had been arranged for Detective Inspector Mark Riley to come with a colleague to look at the safe.

They arrived promptly at seven o'clock. It was getting dark. They had brought a couple of torches with them. Johnny, Katie and I took them round to the shed.

Mark's colleague was a jewellery expert. He looked closely at the area where the paint was missing and did some tests. 'Yes,' he said, 'there is no doubt about it, this part of the safe is definitely almost pure gold.'

'Well spotted,' Mark told us. 'You have done well finding this. Let's all go indoors and you can tell us how and where you found it.'

Johnny's mum and dad joined us in their lounge. We explained how we had more or less been led on a treasure hunt. This had started during a visit we had made to a scrapyard with my auntie Maudie, where Johnny had found a strange-looking message in a car owner's manual in an old Jaguar. And if it had not been for the damaged paintwork on the safe, we might still have been wondering what was so special about it.

Having been told the full story, Mark said he would need to get a research colleague to look into

Charlie Trinder's criminal escapades. This should help us find out who the gold belonged to when it was stolen and who it belonged to now, if anyone. To assist in this, he needed to borrow the by now famous Jaguar owner's manual, and he also asked if he might borrow our decoded messages.

'It might take a week or two to come up with the answer to this question. In the meantime, I think it would be wise if we sent someone to remove the safe from your shed, for safe keeping in a secure police warehouse.'

Johnny's parents were pleased about this. They had had visions of present-day villains finding out that there was a large amount of gold sitting in their not-very-secure shed.

Sunday 10th April

Johnny came to see me after breakfast to tell me that the police had already collected the safe. They had apparently left two police officers by the shed overnight, just in case the word of its existence and whereabouts had already got out.

'I was sad to see it go in a way,' he told me. 'Finding it was such an adventure. I hope we can go on more treasure hunts in the future.'

I agreed that the whole adventure, starting in the scrapyard to finding the safe in Wales, had been the coolest of things imaginable. And to cap it all, finding the gold, hidden in the safe in the way that it was, was the coolest part of all.

Monday 11th April

Back to school again today. In Geography we were asked to choose an area in the UK and write an essay on some of its well-known features. I have decided to write about Wales and its castles. I can include my photo of Harlech Castle. Fortunately, I picked up a booklet about it when we were there last week, which gave lots of information. This will be most helpful.

Friday 15th April

Mark Riley sent me a text message asking if he could pop in tomorrow morning as he had news concerning the safe. I consulted Mum and Johnny and it was agreed that this would be fine. I wonder what he has to tell us.

Saturday 16th April

Mark arrived soon after eleven o'clock. Mum invited him in to have a cup of tea. Katie, Johnny and I joined Mark and Mum in our lounge.

'Well now,' Mark told us. 'I've asked a colleague look into Charlie Trinder's history. Based on the dates when Charlie purchased his car and the date he died in a car crash, my colleague was able to get a rough idea of when the gold must have been stolen. He then looked at our records, which show when large quantities of gold were stolen in the London area. There were four occasions when this happened, but on two of them the gold was quickly recovered. This just left two cases when the gold was never found.'

'So have you pinned our gold down to either of these?' Katie asked.

'Yes,' Mark replied. 'We have contacts in the London gangland underworld. One of these, who has long since retired from crime, was questioned just a day ago. He told us that one of the raids which was never cleared up by us was the work of the Trinder brothers' gang. He admitted he had actually helped the Trinders in that raid, which took place in 1975.'

'Wow that's before you were born, Mum!' I commented.

'Now don't give my age away,' Mum replied,

laughing.

'Our informer-contact is now quite happy to tell us about this crime. Firstly, as he knows the Trinders are all long gone, and secondly as he is hoping to get part of any reward that may be given,' Mark told us.

'Looking at our police records we were never sure how the robbery took place. The gold was on its way in a security van from a large depot near Heathrow airport. It was being transported to a manufacturer of gold medals and sports trophies, like cups and plaques. The van was loaded up and set off with the gold in the form of bullion bars. However, when the van arrived at its destination, it was found to be empty.'

'Didn't the van driver say what had happened to the gold when he arrived?' Johnny asked.

'That's a good question, Johnny. However, the van was left outside the manufacturer's gates minus the driver. He must have left it and done a runner. There were hardly any security cameras in those days so we could find nothing to indicate who was driving, and no fingerprints were found in the van.'

'Our underworld informer told us that, on its way to make the delivery, the van containing the gold entered a tunnel and was driven straight up into the rear of a large pantechnicon. That is, it entered an even larger van. Just before this, an identical van to that, carrying the gold, was reversed out of the pantechnicon, and as the gold-carrying van drove into the tunnel, the lookalike van drove out the other side.'

'Some cool plan!' Johnny cried.

'It's a wonder no one spotted the van driving up into the pantechnicon,' Katie murmured.

'Well, our informant tells us they had a fake police officer posted at the entrance to the tunnel. He was to stop any cars coming and ask to see their driving licences. In the event, no cars arrived during the van-switch operation. In addition, no cars could come in the opposite direction as the crooks had chosen a tunnel which was one-way traffic only. Cars coming in the opposite direction used a second, separate tunnel.'

'A very carefully planned job,' Mum commented. 'However, I don't see why the robbers went to the trouble of having a second van to drive to the medal manufacturers.'

'Well, I think it made for an almost instant disappearance of the gold. Stopping and unloading it into another van would have taken quite a few minutes, which would have increased the chance of them being spotted. Yes, it certainly was a well-planned robbery. We only know the details now because our informant was at the time a member of the Trinder gang.'

'Bit of a cheek if he expects to get a reward,

considering he was one of the original robbers,' Katie commented.

'Yes,' Mark replied, 'I doubt he will get anything. He should have tipped us off straight after the raid, if he seriously wanted rewarding. It's rather late in the day now. It's not as if he found the gold for us – you children did that.'

'So what happens now?' I asked. 'Have you discovered who, if anyone, owns the gold.'

'Whilst the gold was in transit, it was insured by the Kalamazoo Bullion Insurance Company. However, they no longer exist.'

'So does no one own the gold now?' Katie asked.

'Yes, there is a new owner,' Mark replied. 'You see, the Kalamazoo Bullion Insurance Company was taken over by the Rock Island Bullion Insurance Group and they still exist. They have a branch in London and have sent someone to examine the safe. We are waiting to have a report from them.'

Thursday 21st April

This morning I was wondering when we might hear from Mark.

When I got home from school, Mum said Mark had rung and was coming round this evening with a Mr Woodbridge of the Rock Island Bullion Insurance Group, to speak to us.

I phoned Johnny, and he agreed to come round. In fact, he was so excited about it he wanted to come straight away. So I invited him over, saying he could stay for our evening meal, after asking Mum if that was okay. On the dot of 7:30pm, the doorbell rang. It was Mark and Mr Woodbridge.

Mum invited them in. Mark introduced Mr Woodbridge, who was a portly, cheery American.

He told us that the safe had been carefully examined. They had removed the steel door and weighed the rest of the safe, which as we knew was made of gold.

'That safe of yours weighed in at almost three hundredweight imperial, or as you Brits are used to metric measurements, about 150 kg. The gold bars originally stolen weighed just over 175 kg, so it appears some of the gold was dispersed elsewhere following the robbery.'

Mark said, 'It is likely that it was used to pay off gang members that were brought in to help with the robbery. So I think our informer will already have had his quota and will therefore get no more.'

Mr Woodbridge then told us that, when the safe was constructed, the gold in it would have been worth about three hundred and eighty thousand pounds. 'Of course,' he continued, 'gold prices have risen dramatically since that time and we estimate it is now worth around six million pounds.'

We were all quite amazed to think we had found this amount of treasure.

'There was a reward of £500 offered for information leading to finding the gold at the time of the robbery. As the value of gold has risen since then, we consider the appropriate reward for its recovery now would be ten thousand pounds.'

'Well, we didn't go searching for it in order to get a reward,' I told him. 'We did it as a challenge!'

'That's as may be,' Mr Woodbridge replied, 'but the Rock Island Bullion Insurance Group have decided to give you young detectives the whole reward. However, as this is a large sum of money we thought it wise if, for the present, most of it should be put into trust funds for you. Therefore, each of you will be given money in the form of a fund, which will keep it safe until you are eighteen, when you can use it as you feel fit.

'A smaller amount can be given to you now if you have an immediate cash requirement for any reason.'

Mum thought this was a good idea and we agreed

it made sense.

I reminded everyone that we had promised Bronwyn a milking machine if the treasure was found, so the cost of this should be made available. Katie thought we also ought to give Gwen some kind of gift as she had been so helpful. Johnny and I were happy with this.

'That's fine,' Mr Woodbridge told us. He then said that his office would be in touch with us to iron out the details.

After Mark and Mr Woodbridge had gone, we were left in something of a state of shock. However, after talking about it we agreed that, for the time being, we would be little affected, as most of the money was going to be invested for us until we were a good bit older. We had until that time to decide what was best to do with it.

In the meantime, we could buy a milking machine for Bronwyn's cow, Ermintrude, and a small gift for Gwen, Bronwyn's friend.

'Perhaps we should also give our local Neighbourhood Watch Group some money to pay for more items to help keep people safe in the area,' I suggested. These might include front door stickers warning that we had an NHW group, and perhaps shed alarms, as burglaries of things like lawn mowers had recently been on the increase.

Katie and Johnny were happy with this idea.

'And we must not forget Sonia,' I added. 'If it had not been for her we might never have solved the coded message found in the New Forest with its link with Treasure Island.'

'Yes, that's true,' Katie agreed.

'Some gold earrings might be appropriate,' mum suggested.

We all agreed this was a very suitable idea, even though we were unsure how to get them to her at MI5.

Tuesday 26th April

Uncle David has been doing some research for us concerning the purchase of a dairy cow milking machine. He has been in touch with a dairy farmer he knows, and a suitable machine has been recommended. It is very portable, being on wheels. It just needs plugging into an electricity socket and is good to go. He reckons it would be ideal for Bronwyn. It can milk goats as well, so if she wanted to branch out into having a few goats this would also be just the job.

It is quite expensive, but Johnny, Katie and I think she deserves it, having looked after Trinder's golden safe over so many years.

We have received a questionnaire from Mr Woodbridge's company asking how the reward should be paid. Johnny's mum and Katie and mine helped us decide how to fill in the questionnaire. Bearing Bronwyn's milking machine in mind we have asked for enough cash to be sent to pay for this and added another hundred pounds for our local Neighbourhood Watch group. We have also asked for sufficient funds to buy a small gift for Gwen. Mum and Katie think a Welsh Clogau gold dragon pendant necklace would be suitable. This gold comes from the Clogau gold mines in mid-Wales, which are not far from Harlech, and the dragon is a Welsh symbol (there is a red dragon on the Welsh national flag). And finally, we have requested cash to purchase some gold earrings for Sonia. The remainder can go into trust funds for us three children, as discussed with Mr Woodbridge.

Wednesday 27th April

My mum has been in touch with Johnny's mum and the upshot is that we are to have a big joint party. It will be round at the Addison's house this coming Saturday. Not only will it celebrate our successful treasure hunt, but Katie and Johnny have birthdays coming up very soon. Katie will be fourteen this Friday and Johnny eleven one day later, on Saturday. Katie has agreed to delay her share of the party until Saturday, as long as she can open her presents on Friday!

Mum has offered to bake two birthday cakes and Mrs Addison will lay on lots of other party dishes. Auntie Maudie, Uncle David and Gran will be coming and will bring plenty of drinks for both children and adults. It sounds as if it's going to be a great party, in fact close to awesome!

Thursday 28th April

We have been in touch with Detective Inspector Mark Riley and invited him to the party on Saturday. He said he had been sent an item by the Rock Island Insurance Group. It would make an interesting present for one of us children. He was wondering which of us it should be given to. After a little discussion with him, I agreed it should be given to Johnny. He was likely to be the one of us most thrilled with it. Also as it was his find in Trinder's old Jaguar that had set us off on our treasure hunt, he was the person who deserved it most. Mark said he would wrap it up and bring it with him to the party on Saturday.

Saturday 30th April

It's party day. We go round to Johnny's house at two o'clock this afternoon. Katie had her presents yesterday: lots of new clothes and shoes and glitzy nail varnish.

<u>Later</u>

Back home now. Had a great party at Johnny's house. Katie had some of her friends join us and Johnny had a couple of his mates from his school there. I gave him two games for his K-box 10. One was an adventure game which was based on one of his favourite Tintin books, and the second was *Rally Car Racing*. One of the races featured was round the Hafren Forest in Wales. I thought he might like that because we had been there in Connie, when we walked up to the source of the River Severn.

At about 2.30pm, there was a knock on Johnny's front door and in came Mark Riley; he was carrying a large parcel for Johnny. Johnny was very impressed by the size of this present.

'Wow!' he cried. 'It looks awesome.'

Milly, who was with us and had been very quiet up to now, suddenly became very interested in the large package. She had of course been trained to inspect parcels and the like, in her past professional sniffer dog capacity. This amused Mark and he said, 'Just wait until you see what's in here, young madam!'

She wagged her tail and sat patiently.

He then placed it on the floor and asked Johnny if he could guess what it was.

'Well, it looks great,' Johnny replied, 'but golly, it weighs a ton!' He tilted it onto its side to unwrap it. 'Perhaps it's a concrete birdbath for Chippy when he visits!'

We all had to laugh. Auntie Maudie reckoned it was a large barbecue for Johnny, on which he could cook us all sausages later! No one else ventured any suggestions, as it seemed a very odd sort of present. I of course knew what it was, as I had discussed who should have it with Mark on Thursday, but I refrained from saying anything.

Johnny then went to work opening it, which took quite a time, as it was well wrapped up and Millie kept getting in the way trying to help!

At last, when it was uncovered from its wrapping Johnny had to admit it was 'dead cool'!

It was, in fact, the steel door which had been removed from Charlie Trinder's golden safe.

'Ben and I thought you might like it as a reminder of your great treasure hunt,' Mark told Johnny. 'Ben thought that if anyone should have it, it should be you as you were the one to uncover the first coded message.'

'So where are you going to keep it, Johnny?' his mum asked him, looking rather anxious.

'In my bedroom of course,' he replied. 'It could be

fixed to my wall where I could look at it.'

Johnny's dad said he was sure he could fix it so that its weight would be held there firmly.

Auntie Maudie, who had in reality guessed correctly what it was, but hadn't wanted to spoil the surprise, suggested to Johnny's dad that he could cut a bit of wall out behind the safe door for Johnny to keep secret documents in.

Johnny's dad was not keen on this idea, as it would mean damaging the wall and Johnny said he had no secret documents anyway. So that idea was a dead duck as far as they were concerned. However, Johnny said he would like to be able to open the safe door as he had the key for it and knew the lock's combination number.

We all enjoyed the rest of the party as there were lots of eats and drinks and of course the cakes that Mum had baked. Candles were lit on both. Katie and Johnny had a race to see who could blow theirs out the quickest. I think it was a dead heat. Speaking of cake, Chippy made an appearance, tapping on a window to be let in. Fortunately, the cake candles had all been blown out by then, so his feathers did not risk being singed. In the past he has been known to attack a cake when no one was looking! He was now given some cake by Johnny's mum and then settled on top of a cabinet to watch the rest of the proceedings until it was time for us all to go home.

Sunday 1st May

Had a fairly quiet day today. Did revision for exams, which we are having at school this week. Then in the afternoon I went round to Johnny's house. His dad had already fixed the safe door to his bedroom wall. It looked impressive as it had been cleaned up and well-polished. He opened the door for me to see inside. He had stuck a large photo of Trinder's Jag, which I had given him, on the wall behind.

We then played the new games I had given him for his K-Box 10. Later we decided we needed a bit of fresh air, so we took Millie and Chippy to the park.

Saturday 7th May

Well a whole week has gone by, and I have not touched my diary. As I have already mentioned, we have been having exams at school and I have been doing my usual last-minute revision for them.

Lots of other things have been going on at home in the meantime.

On Monday

We received a cheque to cover the cost of Bronwyn's milking machine for Ermintrude and ordered it for delivery direct to Bronwyn's smallholding at Cwmbwlch. We also had another cheque which covered our gifts to the local Neighbourhood Watch, Gwen and Sonia. Mum and I went to the bank and organised a cheque of £100 for the Neighbourhood Watch Committee, care of Major George Banks, their chairman, and cash to purchase a pendant for Gwen and earrings for Sonia.

On Tuesday

I had a letter from the Major, thanking us for the money, which he said would be put to good use keeping the area safe from villains, as he put it. He also said that he hoped Johnny and I would come to their next meeting; they all wanted to hear about our treasure hunt, which had been mentioned briefly in the local newspaper.

On Wednesday
We three children received trust fund certificates from Rock Island as promised, with money invested for us until we are eighteen years old. For safe keeping, Mum put Katie's and my certificates in her lockable fireproof box with other valuable documents. Johnny also received his certificate this morning and has locked it behind his safe door in his bedroom!

On Thursday
Gwen sent us a letter in the morning post, thanking us for the pendant necklace. She said she was thrilled with it. She loves the Clogau jewellery; she has a Clogau ring which her late husband gave her fifteen years ago, shortly before he sadly died.

Yesterday
I had a phone call from Bronwyn. She was very thrilled to have the milking machine as it would speed up her daily work. She was also thinking of getting some goats, as the machine could also milk these. She could then start selling goat milk locally, as there was a

demand for this. In particular, a local cheese factory boss had said they would take all the goats' milk she could spare, as goats' cheese is very popular.

She had realised that we must have traced the gold, otherwise we could not have sent her the milking machine. So we then had a long conversation in which I told her how and where we had found the gold and everything which had happened since we'd last seen her. She was very amused to think that the gold had sat in her shed all those years in plain view. Not that many people had seen in the shed, but it had fooled the two villains who had come searching for the gold all those years ago!

This Morning

Thanks to help from Detective Inspector Mark Riley, it was arranged for me to speak to Sonia on a special phone line. She was thrilled to hear we had found Trinder's gold and was amazed to hear how he had hidden it.

'Well done you and your detective pals,' she commented. 'As your treasure hunt is no longer a secret mission for you, if you don't mind, I will write a piece about it for our staff magazine. I am sure my colleagues in MI5 would enjoy reading about it.'

I agreed that this would be fine and wished her all the best.

I added, 'If you ever need our help again we're ready and willing!'

THE END

Jock

THE AUTHOR was born in India to missionary parents. He attended school at Eltham College and obtained science degrees at Newcastle University and Imperial College London. He worked as a plant and soil consultant for the Minisrty of Agriculture Fisheries and Food and then for its privatised consultancy succesor ADAS. His work took him to various regions of the UK. He is now retired, living in the Vale of Glamorgan. He is married with three sons and two grandchildren. His hobbies include gardening, painting, walking, writing and occasionally playing the saxophone.

Other books by Richard Skinner

The Diary of a Junior Detective, Ben Baxter's Private Diary.

Ben Baxter Investigates the Haunted Vicarage and Other Mysteries.